A

Arpit Vageria is one of India's most loved storytellers. He has penned several bestsellers, including You Are My Reason to Smile, Be My Perfect Ending and I Still Think About You.

Tata Motors made a special documentary around his journey to inspire youngsters to read more. He currently writes for Indian OTT, television and film industry.

He understood that money isn't everything at a very young age and that's when he chose a career of writing books. It might not pay as much, but the satisfaction and happiness he gets is immense.

When he's not writing, he contemplates about his other possible career choices of being a cricketer, singer, actor, historian, traveller or maybe an astronaut one of these days. Being a Tik-Toker hasn't crossed his mind yet.

You can send in your love to him at:

: *arpitvageria401@gmail.com*

: @arpitvageria27

: @arpitvageria

: @arpitvageria27

: +91-8451829595

Praise for the author and his works

'...strikes a chord with Indian readers...'

– *Deccan Chronicle*

'A thrilling romance...well-paced and electric...'

– *The Times of India*

'A perfect read.'

– *Rashtradoot*

'...attempts to soothe Pak-India relations, his writings are perfectly unbiased and omniscient throughtout. His novels spur harmony and goodwill.'

– *Dawn (Pakistan)*

'Arpit Vageria sells love through words...'

– *First Print*

'Arpit wants to make reading more appealing...'

– *The Hindu*

Gift Me a New Beginning

Believe in Love...

Arpit Vageria

ARPIT VAGERIA

Srishti
PUBLISHERS & DISTRIBUTORS

Srishti Publishers & Distributors
A unit of AJR Publishing LLP
212A, Peacock Lane
Shahpur Jat, New Delhi – 110 049
editorial@srishtipublishers.com

First published by
Srishti Publishers & Distributors in 2022

10 9 8 7 6 5 4 3 2 1

This is a work of fiction. The characters, places, organisations and events described in this book are either a work of the author's imagination or have been used fictitiously. Any resemblance to people, living or dead, places, events, communities or organisations is purely coincidental.

All stories included in this book have been individually published as ebooks.

Printed and bound in India

Dedicated to all my readers,
my extended family,
who made me what I am today.
This book is specifically
for each one of you.

A note to my readers

Hello, my dear reader!

Can you believe it's already ten years that we have known each other? Wow!

I've not met a lot of you personally, but someday, I really wish to. That's one thing I'd like to do before I breathe my last. Each one of you is a family member I've never met. Kind of my last wish, let's say.

This is a special note of love and gratitude for you, for believing in me all these years and continuing your faith in me to deliver one story after another. This is my seventh book, but the love I've received is from millions.

I never thought I'd write again after my last note to you. I had decided to not write any more love stories till the time I saw for myself that love still exists in this world. After reading that note, I received more than twenty-five thousand messages from my readers from across the world, asking me to not stop writing love stories.

When I read some small, some long but such emotional messages, saying that my stories had made them believe in love in the first place, it made me re-think my decision.

I kind of found it unfair to give up writing midway, when this world needed it the most. I might or might not be able to make much of a difference to everyone's journey, but even if a few people out of millions believe in love because of me, I'll feel that my mission has been accomplished.

In all honesty, that is one of the prime reasons why I started writing again, but here's something not many know! I recently lost my god, my grandfather, Late Sohanlalji Vageria. He always believed in love and only believed in spreading love amongst people.

16th February 2021 was my sister Shikha's wedding. I went to Pratapgarh in Rajasthan and met Dadaji there. He was 92. He still remembered everything about my childhood, my wife Pooja and asked me about the baby we were going to welcome next month. He promised me twice that he'll visit Indore to meet the baby and cried when he promised me the second time, as if he knew he won't be able to make it.

I held his hand, and started crying myself. I knew that he was here for a few more weeks, but I didn't want to face the reality. I knew that the day would be here anytime, and soon, but he promised again before I left. I kissed his hands, hugged him for one last time as he asked me, '*Kyo ja raha hai itni jaldi*?' I had no answer to it. I kept watching him till the last second and we welcomed Mayra on 27th February 2021.

I wanted to go and fulfill his wish of meeting Mayra, but Covid caught me and my family one after another. As we recovered from it just before mid-April, we decided to go and meet him with Mayra in a few days.

On 20th April 2021 at around midnight, his health deteriorated. As we left from Indore to meet him at Pratapgarh, time won the race and I lost my Dadaji. He couldn't meet Mayra. I lost the person who loved me the most. I lost the person who made me believe in love. I lost the person who's the reason behind my united family.

I cursed myself for not reaching there a few hours earlier and this regret is always going to stay with me. I have his cap, his old watch which is almost seventy years old, his notebook and his handkerchief. I still smell it and it reminds me of him. Daily. That's how I start my day. I feel like he's around.

He appeared in my dream a few months later and with a smiling face, he told me, 'Don't worry beta! I met Mayra. She's a happy kid and very beautiful.' It felt so real. It felt like a message to me, so that I could move on. I still see him in my dreams sometimes, and I wish to see him in my dreams forever, because dreams do come true someday. And I believe that I'll meet him once again, someday.

His love didn't die for me, even after his death. And my love didn't die for him either. It just increased manifold.

I am going to continue my belief in love and spread love like my Dadaji did. I am going to write many more love stories because he always used to be my first reader and I truly believe that he'll read this story too, wherever he is.

To this and many more to come. Cheers!

Yours,
Arpit Vageria

1
Happy Anniversary

Three days after his anniversary, Roshan decided to visit his old flat. He had wanted to go on the special day itself, but knowing that it could land him in trouble, he changed his mind. So today, he picked his favourite coconut lychee crush from 'The Jungle Juice, Kandivali' and bought a cake from the nearby bakery to celebrate the occasion.

He looked unrecognizable in his recently-changed look. He was looking neat, well-dressed and a lot unlike his usual self. He eagerly waited for this day, just like every other year.

He looked at his diary for one last time before he boarded a cab. He saw something as he settled down in the cab and smiled.

'OTP sir,' the cabbie asked.

'2927,' Roshan replied, looking at the cake lovingly. He noticed that the bakery guy had written in cursive handwriting – "Happy anniversary". He asked the cabbie to wait and rushed back to the bakery.

He saw the man behind the counter and almost screamed, 'You spoiled the cake! I specifically asked you to mention "Happy Birthday". And you wrote "Happy Anniversary" instead!'

'Sir, I remember you asked me to write Happy Anniversary.' The employee named Deepak said in an animated voice, that seemed to express concern. Though in reality, it just meant he was least interested in this trivial concern.

'You can't fool an oldie. You can't loot me like this!' Roshan said angrily.

With that, he picked up his phone and started dialling his grandson's number. The number was continuously busy, which frustrated Roshan, and also the employee. He kept trying for ten long minutes.

By this time, the cab driver was also there, asking if he should leave. There was silence, but utter chaos. 'Sir, I've been waiting for more than ten minutes. Do you want me to drop you or not?'

'I am paying you to wait, so please wait. I am just fixing certain things here. This bakery guy has deceived me. I am going to make it right,' he said in an overdramatic tone, which he had heard so often in English movies. The British accent would have been hard to miss, if not for these simpletons around him.

The cabbie shook his head, frustrated that he was stuck.

'You wait till I get this right, young man,' the old man said. Suddenly, his phone rang. His grandson had finally called back!

'Hi Dadu, what happened? You have been calling and calling… are you okay?'

'Hello Mr Deshpande!… No, I am not fine. There's this bakery guy who's trying to loot me. I thought I should directly inform the police about this.'

Roshan's grandson Shaurya understood that his grandpa was up to something. He was even using his baritone voice to talk like an actual police officer. The trick worked and the bakery guy had to give in to his demand. He offered a complimentary cake in return.

Muttering under his breath, Roshan took both the cakes and headed towards the waiting cab.

The moment he settled in, he received a text from Shaurya.

Hope you got your free cake, Dadu. But please stop fooling people now.

He smiled as he read this message.

The surprised cabbie confirmed the location twice before starting the cab to avoid any confusion or free ride.

Roshan said clearly, 'JB Nagar. I am not going to repeat it. My memory is better than youngsters of today.'

The cabbie offered to switch on the AC, but Roshan refused. Instead, he opened the windows. As the cab entered JB Nagar in the next twenty-five minutes, a smile appeared on his face and he radiated child-like innocence. As soon as he reached his destination, he opened the door and started moving towards a building with a cake in his hand.

The cab driver noticed that the old man had forgotten the other cake in his cab.

He rushed to him and said sarcastically, 'Sir, your memory isn't as great as you think. You've forgotten the other cake in my car.'

'I haven't forgotten anything. That cake is for you. I saw your birth date on your hanging ID card. A very happy birthday to you!' The old man said and smiled. The cabbie looked very shocked at the surprising turn of events.

The old man entered the forty-five-year-old building that had green algae all over its structure. It had many rustic windows that hadn't really changed since the seventies. Far away, there was a marble chair that was also covered with algae.

There were no watchmen to look after the building. It had huge open parking spaces, unlike any other building in Mumbai. Roshan took out the bunch of keys that had "Flat no. 2, Varsha Society" written on it.

He opened the flat and entered, switching on the lights and fan. Then, he filled a glass of water for himself and sat down on the sofa. It seemed like daily routine for him.

He washed his face and applied hair wax to set his hair. He gave himself one last look before starting the celebration.

He opened the cake and just as he was about to slice through it with a knife, he realized he hadn't put on music. He played his favourite song on his phone and started dancing – alone. *Wo pehli baar, jab hum mile* echoed in the room.

While cutting the cake, he imagined that his wife was holding his hand. Every time they used to cut the cake here together, they'd always fight on who'd blow the candles first.

He looked at the marble chair from the window and thought back fondly on how many hours of his life he had spent sitting there. While ruminating, he remembered that even back then, his wife always had some or the other complaint against him.

She wasn't very fond of him, he would say. It was just like any other usual arranged marriage, where a wife would stay in a relationship because leaving a marriage in between would raise many eyebrows. But he loved his wife indefinitely, and he realized it even more once she was gone.

Roshan always felt that he was more connected to things than people. He was drawn to the idea of travelling back in time. He always felt that trees heard him more than humans. The streets talked to him more than his friends and music understood him more than the family. He wasn't mentally sick; he was just a very emotional man who associated things with his life deeply.

His wife always complained that even during their marriage, Roshan preferred to live in the past and not in the present. He would reminisce about their beautiful past, but would never try to make his present beautiful. Probably, that was the reason he felt he wasn't loved by his wife as much.

But getting back to the cake in front of him, he cut and ate two pieces – one for himself and the other one for his wife.

'Happy anniversary, Neeru. We would've celebrated our sixtieth anniversary together today.'

He settled down on a chair and opened his diary. He looked up at the clock and realized that it was time for him to go. He packed the cake, cleared the floor and switched off the lights and fans. As he closed the door, he looked around to see if anyone had noticed him coming or going.

As he came to the ground floor lobby, his eyes went to the name plate board. "Varun Sharma and Aditi Sharma" flashed on a piece of paper in front of flat no. 2. He pulled off the paper and revealed the original names written there – "Roshan and Neeru".

He saw those names and smiled.

As he was moving out, he saw a couple entering flat no. 2. He overheard their conversation where the wife was saying. 'Varun, we need to plan a nice surprise for Mayra's birthday.'

As they stepped inside, he heaved a sigh of relief.

At the age of eighty-five, he felt less loved than he deserved. But he clearly remembered the words of his dying wife:

> *Life is all about what it is and not about what it was. I am going to be a part of your past and you'd probably start loving me more than you ever did. But I suggest that this time, you focus on 'What it is'. Remember, it's never too late to be loved.*

But, as his wife had rightly guessed, Roshan was stuck in the past. A past that was filled with regrets, happiness and a pinch of hope that someday, he would be loved the way he deserved.

After looking at his and Neeru's name for one last time, Roshan hailed an auto-rickshaw.

'Bandra,' he said to the auto driver. The auto-rickshaw moved rapidly, taking him to his destination.

2
The Startling News

December brings winter to various parts of India. However, winters in Mumbai always mean less humidity and lesser heat. Mumbaikars enjoy the pleasant weather in December more than any other time of the year.

Around this time, life looks a little less stressed. People love to sip coffees in their balconies and enjoy themselves with their family and friends. That way, December becomes a month of get-togethers, sharing smiles, planning the year-end eve and thinking back on the year – of "What could have been?"

One particular street in Hiranandani township has always belonged to the elite and influential in Mumbai. A place that loved to flaunt not just their status, but also the bonds they share with fellow neighbours, through thick and thin.

This had been a gated society for a long time, so the people here enjoyed the privilege of socializing with others like them. But due to the updated Brihanmumbai Municipal Corporation (BMC) guidelines, they had to open it for others as well. The outsiders who entered this township would often be astonished at how perfect this society was!

But the people of *Beverly Hills* township were not happy. The news flashing on all major channels that morning was going to change their lives forever.

To top it all, a dung-cake seller, who was crossing the street on a motorbike, mistakenly dropped a few pieces of kerosene-filled dung cakes in front of Agarwals' house. Nobody had noticed it yet, but there was more drama to come!

The Agarwals were looking furiously at the news channel screen, as if it was the poor television's fault. Finally, it was the Sachdevas who initiated the conversation with the Agarwals. The Kanitkar family was anyway waiting for someone to start the same discussion. Aroras were visibly frustrated and were cursing the City Mayor, Sridharan, who was the resident and secretary of this township previously.

Arora threw his half-empty cigarette on the road in disgust, which lit up the kerosene-soaked dung cake piece. It caught fire and smoke started coming out of it.

All of them entered Agarwals' residence and started talking about the issue at hand. Suddenly, they turned at the noise and looked at the auto-rickshaw that had just stopped in front of Kothari's residence. Roshan Kothari stepped out of the auto.

Roshan looked around and saw a crowd gathered at the Agarwals'. Surprisingly, most of them were wearing white. Then he saw the smoke emanating from the dung cake. He saw Agarwal's mother; she wasn't wearing a bindi. Then, he saw the most emotional guy on the street, Lakhan Agarwal, who looked shattered. He could cry any moment.

Roshan, as a responsible neighbour and a concerned human being, went to Lakhan and hugged him tightly.

'You don't need to cry, Lakhan. He was a great man! He lived his life like a king. He made us all proud. Remember him for all the great work he has done. He was already very sick in the last few years. God knows how much he was coughing. Thank god for releasing him from his pain. You know beta, he's in a better place now,' Roshan said it all in one go.

That's when he heard loud noises of coughing once again. He looked around and saw people staring at him. Then he saw senior Agarwal standing in the balcony above, sipping his tea and coughing, like always.

'I am not going anytime soon, Roshan!' The old man, who Roshan had presumed to be dead, spoke.

'Wow, that was a strange sequence of events in combination. Why the hell are you all wearing white? What's with those dung cakes? And this crowd here? Lakhan was almost crying and his mother was not wearing any bindi. I am sorry for the misunderstanding, but all this made me presume…' Roshan said, trying to avoid eye contact with anyone.

Then he looked at Lakhan and asked confused, 'But why are you looking so morose, Lakhan?'

'Because I think our street will soon be teeming with criminals. And we won't be able to do anything to stop it!' he spoke at last, all his angst poured into his agonized words.

'All thanks to the Mayor, Sridharan!' Mr Pradeep Kanitkar stated the obvious in a stern voice.

'This isn't the first time Sridharan has tried to create a ruckus in our lives,' Manav Arora roared. He was a young businessman listed amongst the top 50 under 50. 'He made it an open society from a gated one. He also sued the builder for illegal extension. He has done enough to make our lives a living hell. But this time, he has crossed all limits! We can't let this happen. After all, the future of our children is at stake.'

'Our entire township has been known for peace, happiness and solidarity for all these years. If this happens, it will only be known for crimes, murders and thefts. We can't let that happen. We can't give in to the unusual decision taken by Sridharan,' Rahil Sachdeva said. He was the younger son of Mr Vikas Sachdeva, who was a popular TV face, known for his role in a family political drama.

'We should rightfully protest it,' he said it with the same authority as his character Arjun would have said it.

After hearing what everyone had to say, Roshan asked, 'What is this about?'

'Arey Kothari ji, our street will now have a "Correction centre" or as our Mayor would like to call it – a detention centre! Here, the serious criminals, who have completed their punishment in jail, would be living for one year. This centre aims at helping in the transition for them to be accepted into the society, like before,' Lakhan Agarwal said. His house was just next to Sridharan's old house, which was now ready to be converted into a correction centre called 'Prayas'.

'Okay! And why are we scared?' Roshan asked.

'Should we celebrate instead? Happy that criminals will be living with us,' Rahil said sarcastically. 'Uncle, it is common sense! Why don't you get it? People like us can't live with criminals. This is a high-class society.'

Roshan smiled, but said nothing. People around him, who otherwise loved him for his humour, found his smile quite annoying today. With tempers already flaring, this was too much!

'Now you're smiling! I am not sure if I've cracked a joke here, uncle,' Rahil said, throwing his hands up in disappointment. As usual, he was over-acting.

'No, you haven't! But that's what we do, right? We don't accept new things easily. We always love to go by our past experiences. We want the best people to lead our nation, but when we see people like Sachin Tendulkar joining politics, we get critical of them and say – "Why are good guys joining politics, they'll also become dirty." We later crib about not having enough good political leaders.

'That's what we do with criminals as well. We never give them a second chance to be accepted back into the society. This further alienates them and gives them all the more reason to continue with unlawful activities,' Roshan explained.

'This isn't making any sense to me,' Rahil said. Everyone present there nodded in agreement with him.

'Maybe, but according to me, bad guys might have minimal chances to turn over a new leaf while living with good people. But they might never become civilized citizens if they continue living with criminals forever. Remember, this is the programme they chose for themselves. They could've opted out of it, if they wished to. It isn't compulsory to go to the correction centre. It's still a new concept for us in India. Let's give it some time and not be so judgmental,' Roshan said.

He looked around and saw everyone; they did not look convinced. 'However, if you all feel that we should be taking up this matter in front of Sridharan, I'll be the one to lead,' Roshan added and everyone finally smiled.

'But could you all please tell me, why are you all wearing white when that old man is still alive?' he said. They all smiled while the old man tried to laugh, only ending up coughing in the end.

This was the street where people loved and respected each other. They might have disagreed with each other at times, but they always stood up for each other at the end of the day.

This was about to change – forever.

As Roshan entered his house, he stopped by, washed the nameplate with water and rubbed it to make it more visible – "Roshan and Neeru".

There was a sudden downpour, indicating the storm that was waiting for all of them.

3
Not Good Enough

'It's over, Shaurya,' Mehr said, struggling to gather all the shopping bags in her hands. She tried opening the car door, but it wouldn't budge.

'Open the damn child lock, Shaurya!' she said and looked visibly frustrated at the situation.

'But you're my baby, right?' Shaurya said.

'I am not your baby anymore,' Mehr said with a tone of finality in her voice. When Shaurya didn't open the door, she rolled the window down and stretched her hand to open it from outside. She put everything together and started moving towards a rickshaw.

Shaurya got down from his car quickly, locked it and started chasing Mehr. People started honking because in less than one minute, there was a massive traffic jam behind his car. Shaurya was in a fix – he noticed the frustrated people who were honking so that he could move away and then, saw his two-year-old relationship walking away with a dozen shopping bags in her hands. Just like any sincere lover, he decided to chase his girlfriend and let the car create more trouble for people.

'Andheri?' she asked an auto-walla and he denied.

She kept asking many auto-wallas but some said no, some didn't reply and the rest of them just stared at her beautiful body. Mehr finally decided to move towards the local train station. Shaurya was half hoping she'd stop, but she went on. As Shaurya entered inside the crowded station, he saw hundreds of people walking towards him. He had heard about the rush in local trains, but this was the first time he was seeing it first-hand.

He kept chasing her and tried his best to convince her to not leave him. From buying her ticket from the station counter to almost entering a local train coach that had no space, he walked an extra mile to prove his love for her.

They somehow managed to get inside. Mehr entered like a pro, but Shaurya fought a great deal to get inside.

'Why do you even want to break up with me?' he asked. 'What happened?'

'What happened?! Tell me, what have you done for me till date?' Mehr asked. As she said this, Shaurya looked at the shopping bags which had more than thirty branded clothes which he had bought for his girlfriend before she announced a break-up. He thought of talking about the kind of money he spent in his defense, but decided against it. He knew it would only make it worse.

'I just risked my life getting into this local train. Some guy just touched me inappropriately, maybe satiating his soul. And you're asking what have I done for you till date?' Shaurya said in a bid to calm her down. He moved, trying his best to find a small space to place his foot which had till now been mid-air.

He overheard two guys who were cursing each other for touching inappropriately. They were calling each other names. This was something Shaurya was experiencing for the first time in his life.

They were fighting at the top of their voices, because of which, Shaurya just couldn't talk to Mehr about their relationship.

'Can we please get down at some café and discuss it, for old time's sake? I am feeling a little out of place here,' he finally spoke.

'I've got nothing to talk about, Shaurya. It is over. I can't fool myself every single day. I am just not in love with you,' she spoke with conviction.

'Why? Everything was fine between us till a few minutes back! I've never cheated on you. I've got you everything that you ever needed or asked for. How can things change overnight?' he asked her.

'Nothing has changed overnight, Shaurya. It's been happening for a while,' she said. A eunuch, who was asking for money from everyone, was also the source of entertainment in the coach. The eunuch was touching those people inappropriately who weren't giving money.

'What's been happening for a while? What's your problem with me?' Shaurya said and all this while, the eunuch kept touching him to ask for money. Shaurya had to try really hard to ignore all this.

'Bhagwan tum dono ki jodi ko salamat rakhe,' the eunuch said.

'You're pathetic in bed, Shaurya!' she shouted. As she uttered those words, the focus of the people in the coach, which was on the eunuch and the two men fighting, suddenly shifted to what Mehr had just said.

The eunuch thought it appropriate to just go away from there.

'You can't make me feel horny. You can't make me reach an orgasm. Forget about an orgasm, even before I get into the mood, you are done! Maggi is better than you. At least it takes two minutes to cook,' Mehr said.

With that, a lot of people started booing Shaurya. It was free entertainment on a crowded local train!

Shaurya felt a boner from a man who was standing just beside him. Shaurya gave him an angry look and thankfully, the guy was quick to understand.

Mehr looked unapologetic about what she had said. Shaurya, who looked heartbroken, ashamed and guilty, had nothing to say. The train was getting into a station and Shaurya couldn't wait to get down. But before that, he wanted to do something that would hurt Mehr and he did that!

He took all of the shopping bags from Mehr, along with her iPhone and iPad that she was carrying.

'I am just taking what's mine in less than two minutes,' Shaurya said. He started moving away before he turned and said those final words.

'For me, two minutes of love is better than hours of lust. I loved you so sincerely, but you kept judging me for my so-called *performance*! I didn't know I was a reality show contestant and you were the judge,' Shaurya said, giving Mehr some burns, using not only his words, but also the gifts that he took away before getting down.

As Shaurya shed tears in an auto-rickshaw, heading back to where his car was parked, he kept reminding himself that he wasn't wrong. Maybe he wasn't great in bed, but he surely was better than those who only wanted her in bed.

He kept looking at couples around him, chatting happily on the roadsides. It kept reminding him about his relationship with Mehr, which had fallen apart after so many years. He reached the spot where he had left his car and saw a lady traffic constable.

'I'm sorry I had to leave the car midway. It was something urgent,' Shaurya said.

'Yes, that I can see!' the lady inspector said, looking at all of the shopping bags he was carrying. 'You'll have to pay the challan for obstructing traffic intentionally.'

'This is for you. Please let me go. I just broke up with my girlfriend,' Shaurya said and handed over all the shopping bags to the lady.

She looked surprised as no one had ever offered her anything like that. As Shaurya started his car, the words "You're pathetic in bed" kept ringing in his head.

Without even thinking about it, he scrolled back to his old chats with Mehr.

You're a great kisser, you make me feel complete, you're the one for me… and all those lovely messages that are sent when you're in a relationship. He kept reading and rereading his chats with Mehr, but never understood where it had all gone wrong.

He deleted their pictures and all the messages in their chat. He wanted to throw away all the gifts she had ever given him. But sadly, he couldn't! He realized that he had never received any gifts from her.

But the words "You're pathetic in bed" weren't going to leave him so easily.

4
Blend of Both Worlds

People across Mumbai were divided on this decision by the city Mayor. Some of them were calling it a "master move" before the elections, and the rest of them were calling it a "nonsensical thing" to get some advantage over a section of people.

The residents of Beverly Hills were calling it some sort of a deal with the builder, wherein he'd be allowed to retain the illegal extension to his house.

Finally, after a lot of requests, mayor Sridharan agreed to meet the residents of Beverly Hills. As expected, the meeting was futile. Sridharan, who was once a resident of this township, raised his claim of owning his villa. He said that no one had any right to stop him as he could use it the way he wanted.

They all struggled to prove their point, even though they knew the answer. When the residents asked him to shift his correction centre elsewhere, his mouth contorted a little, almost sluggishly. Then, he shook his head and said, 'I granted your request years ago, when you all had asked me to shift my massage centre elsewhere. Now, you want me to shift this too? Not possible!'

'It wasn't a massage centre. It was a villa where you promoted illegal prostitution,' Rahil said.

'Yes, where your father was a regular visitor before he died!' Sridharan replied as he looked intently into Rahil's eyes.

Rahil looked furious and blood rushed to his head. The mayor's words brought him pain and before he could vent his anger, Sridharan added, 'Just focus on your TV show! I've heard that a lot of TV actors do drugs. It will take me no time to prove that it is right. By the way, stop teaching me about law and order. That might be your *interest,* but it's my *job*. I know it better.'

'Sri, we all are concerned about our kids and families. Don't you think it's unfair to just bombard us with your decision of bringing criminals into the society?' Roshan spoke politely, presenting the argument confidently.

'Roshan ji, I respect you a lot, but I also expect you to understand that we don't necessarily like all our neighbours, right? Agarwals didn't like me when I was there, and I didn't enjoy being around them either. Just treat them like another neighbour and *then* make your perception, maybe?'

He waited as he looked around, but focused his words on Roshan the most. 'They've been given a year's relief in their punishment because of their excellent behaviour.' For the very first time in the meeting, he talked with mutual respect. Most definitely because he always respected Roshan the most.

'That's sounding like a one-way conversation to me, Sri, not a discussion,' Roshan spoke. 'That's not why we are here.'

'I never guaranteed that you'll be given what you came for,' Sridharan said as he signed some documents that were given to him by the staff.

'How can you do this to the society where you once lived?' Lakhan said.

'This is ridiculous! I don't understand why we've been talking about my private villa. With the audacity with which you are speaking, it sounds like you're the owner and I've illegally captured your property! This isn't the kind of *discussion* I expected,' Sridharan said in a soft voice, but flashed that vicious smile that no one liked.

'Nonetheless, I suggest that you keep your preparations ready for the new neighbours. They're coming soon. They would be happy to see a grand welcome in the new neighbourhood,' he added and waved his hand – his typical gesture to end the conversation as he excused himself from the meeting.

The people from the happiest neighbourhood in town were looking rather tensed. The faces that once smiled the most had lines of worry on their foreheads. Those who once talked about making strangers their own, were worried for their own kin now. The neighbourhood that was known for its peace was worried about their harmony getting distorted. And the people who loved their freedom were already feeling caged in their own houses.

The blend of two different worlds was about to happen. And the world knows – whenever two contrasting worlds have come together in the past, the results have been disastrous.

5

The Grand Welcome

Roshan and Shaurya were sitting on their well-designed terrace that had sitting areas, a garden area and enough place to do their occasional bonfire on those cool December nights. It was one of those things that Shaurya always loved doing with his grandfather. When he was young, he had seen his father and grandfather doing the same over drinks. They'd laugh, cry and dine beside that bonfire.

He had observed his father's fascination for old things. His father would always ask Roshan about the places he had lived in, the kind of schools they used to have and what sort of neighbours did they have when Roshan was young. Shaurya's father Soham had an enormous amount of interest in knowing about the things bygone. That's one habit that Shaurya had inherited from his father, and his father had inherited from his grandfather.

Shaurya looked at Roshan; he was pouring himself a glass of wine. He kept putting big logs to heat the bonfire, just how his father always liked.

'Missing Papa?' Shaurya asked.

'That's a routine for the last ten years now,' Roshan said as he smiled and adjusted the logs more. He signalled Shaurya to sit.

'So, how did your cake thing go? Why did you want it for free, Dadu?'

'I wanted to gift it to the cab driver. It was his birthday.'

'You have enough money to feed that cab driver and his family for a lifetime! Why did you pull that poor baker's leg for free?' Shaurya asked.

'I love cheap thrills!' Roshan had a twinkle in his eye. 'That keeps me alive. Moreover, I will make up to the baker some other day, in another way. If there's anything that your grandmother ever liked about me, it was these small things.'

'You would still not give up, right? You're still trying to impress her. It's been more than twenty years since she has gone, Dadu.'

'These twenty years have passed quicker than the forty years that we spent together,' Roshan said and Shaurya laughed.

'How could she not fall in love with me during those forty years of our marriage?' Roshan questioned himself.

'Sometimes you're just not compatible enough for the other person,' Shaurya said with a sigh.

'Or maybe you don't *want to be* compatible with the other person for some reason.'

'What sort of reason?' Shaurya asked, curious.

'You don't need a reason to not be compatible. All you need is an excuse.'

'What was her excuse, Dadu?'

'Before I could find out, she was gone forever. I kept chasing her to know what was not working. But I never got an answer to the question I had asked sixty years ago. Love doesn't have a definition as such, but even if it did, it would be just that love is the wait that has no destination. Of course, a popular definition would also be - that love means never having to say you're sorry!'

'Hmm. But when did it stop working for you two?'

'It never started working. To be frank, I kept trying to make some places, our places; some songs, our songs; and some evenings, our evenings. In my head, I was creating memories, but I'd never know the reality. It's gone with her. Sometimes love asks for sacrifices. It gets worse when it asks for sacrificing your own love.' As Roshan confessed this out loud to his grandson, there were tears in his eyes, despite the smile on his face. That's the thing with old people. They'll bring the world to you and wouldn't even let you know of the pain they've gone through.

There was silence for a few seconds, and in those few seconds, Roshan kept looking at the burning logs in the bonfire. He kept looking at the intensity of it and shifted his chair a couple of inches back as the heat started getting unbearable.

'How much did you love her, Dadu?'

'As much as she probably hated me.'

'How much did she love you?'

'Multiply anything by zero and you'll get the answer,' Roshan replied after giving it some thought.

'How can someone hate the one who loves them so much?' Shaurya asked, confused.

'You're talking about barter here. There's no barter in love. If it is equal from both sides, it's not true love. Rather, it's like a business deal.'

'Did you ever feel loved by her, at any point in time?' Shaurya's curiosity rose with every word.

'Yes!'

'When?'

'When she was dying. When she was in my arms and there was no one else for her.'

'How do you know?'

'The way she was closing her eyes, I saw her hatred towards me fading away. Her complaints were also dying with her. She probably wanted a moment with me before she breathed her last. It felt like she wanted to end everything on a happy note so that if we meet someday in some world, we wouldn't have any grudges against each other. She smiled which seemed to convey – "I couldn't love you enough, forgive me for that." I am sure if I get another life with her, I'll surely impress her, but sometimes an apology hurts more than the mistake, because it takes you back to where it all started. While going back in the past could give you hope or pain, but in my case, hope died with the person who apologized and I was left hurt.'

Roshan said and picked up the wine bottle to fill Shaurya's wine glass.

'Were you pathetic in bed? Could that be a reason?' Shaurya asked.

Roshan stopped pouring the wine suddenly; his hands froze in place. He looked around awkwardly and then, asked Shaurya, 'What did you just ask me?'

'Don't let me repeat it, Dadu. I have gathered enough courage to ask you this once already.'

'Forget about courage, why would you ask me this in the first place?'

'I thought we were trying to be friends here?'

'And you took it way too seriously.'

'I always take your advice seriously.'

Roshan felt quite uncomfortable at what Shaurya had just asked. He couldn't even look into his twenty-five-year-old grandson's eyes. Yes, there were times when he wanted to be friends with Shaurya so that he didn't miss his parents so much. And then there were times like these, where he regretted becoming so frank with him.

They both knew that there was a wind of discomfort between them. To brush it off, Shaurya said, 'I broke up with my girlfriend today. I mean, my girlfriend broke up with me today because she thinks I am pathetic in bed.'

'How many times have you... you know, been with her?' Roshan asked, looking elsewhere, feeling awkward.

'Now you're trying to be friends with me,' Shaurya answered.

'Shut up and answer, okay?'

'Four-five times.'

'Not a big deal! This kind of intimacy takes time! Virat Kohli too started performing in cricket only from his sixth innings. She needs to give you time. What's the hurry?'

'I am a T-20 player and she wants someone who is good at test matches. So, she's not in a hurry. I am in a hurry... if you know what I mean.'

'I surely know what you mean. No need to get into the details or be ashamed of it,' he said and paused midway.

'Should I take some medication and then approach her?'

'No need! You're too young to go the medicine way. I still don't need it. And I don't buy her reason, honestly!'

'Why would you need it *now*? Oh wait! Are you still...?' Shaurya said over-dramatically.

'No, no, no! Stop your mind from imagining wild things.'

'Don't be such a creepy old man, Dadu.'

'Oh, shut up!'

'I can't do this; I can't do that. What's the solution then?' Shaurya asked.

'Just let it be! Stop worrying about what happened today with your girlfriend. Live in the present moment.'

'Says the person who still smells Dadi's old saree and keeps checking his wedding album every now and then. More than me, you're the one who lives in the past.' Shaurya said and a thought suddenly lit up his face. 'Dadu, you sound like a person who'd never give up on love.'

'One shouldn't.'

'Then, why are you giving up on love now?' Shaurya said as he put another log into the fire. He picked up Roshan's mobile phone and started fidgeting with it.

'What are you up to now?' Roshan asked pointing at his mobile. Shaurya showed him the screen where he had just downloaded a dating app called 'Binge Date' and created Roshan's profile.

A message popped up on the screen. '*Congrats, you're the youngest at heart person on our application. Love is ageless and you've proved it. Good luck finding love.*'

'Have you gone nuts? You want me to find love at the age of 85?'

'You just said love is ageless. This app too believes in it. Forget about the age and just look at a few people who're ready for meeting you. Never say never, Dadu! No harm in trying, right?'

'No matter how much you try to sell me this garbage of an idea, I am definitely not getting into it. I don't know, but it sounds like someone selling a packet of condoms to me,' Roshan said with gross expressions and a disgusted face.

'What the hell!' Shaurya said and made a face. They sort of competed in making faces. 'Ewwwww, how can you even think like that?' Shaurya said.

'It's time you live in the present, Dadu. Stop assuming; start living in the present,' Shaurya said as after a few awkward reactions, they finally settled down. That is when they heard some sirens.

As they sat melting away their blues in the bonfire, a blue-coloured police van entered the street. The sirens had been blaring from a distance and were quite loud by now. The police van stopped at Sridharan's villa and the prisoners started stepping out of it.

'Not just me... seems like there are other people who prefer to live in the past. Looks like Sridharan is taking revenge for the old tiff,' Roshan said.

Almost everyone was out of their villas now. What looked like a grand welcome by a crowd wasn't welcoming at all. Rather, it was their sheer fear that forced them to step out to see their new neighbours, who were going to be there for a while now.

The Kotharis remembered how this street had welcomed them a few decades back. The Aroras recollected how they were made to feel at home when they shifted here from Delhi. Agarwals, who were the oldest on the street, remembered how they got along so well with the Kanitkars during their early days. But no one on this street remembered when any new neighbour was given such a cold welcome at their arrival.

Their expressions screamed that they weren't happy with what they were watching. But that's what chess is about. The ability to check-mate is in the hands of the one who stays in power. You lose some games, you win some; but they were determined to win this one at any cost. After all, their home was in danger! Their families were on the line of fire.

6
A Strange Friendship

A few days after 'Prayas' opened, seeing a police van in the street became routine. People who used to jog in the mornings and evenings either changed their route, or stopped jogging completely. The property rates of Beverly Hills nosedived suddenly and drastically. The roadside stalls of pani-puri and cigarette vendors started occupying spaces temporarily, which irked the society members.

The colony that once boasted of housing businessmen, millionaires, actors and all other high society members, now had rapists, murderers, thieves and different types of law-breakers.

Seven males and three females were staying in the correction centre at present. They would roam like regular citizens and use all the facilities given by the society. Officially, they were still tenants provided by the state government. According to city safety surveys, Beverly Hills – which was once rated one of the safest places to live in Mumbai – was now considered one of the most dangerous places to reside.

Shaurya stopped by the cigarette vendor one evening. He asked for Davidoff cigarettes, but the vendor didn't have it. A girl passing by stopped there too.

'Classic Milds *milega. Chalega tumko? Jaldi batao*?' The cigarette vendor gave Shaurya a now or never offer.

'Looks like you have good taste,' the girl spoke.

'I won't deny that. However, I started with Davidoff because it sounded cool. And now that I cannot quit smoking, I thought of continuing my friendship with Davidoff,' Shaurya replied.

'Friendship with cigarettes is dangerous,' she said sweetly.

'I don't think so! If not for cigarettes, what else would've made you talk to me? Right?' Shaurya said with a charming smile pasted on his face.

'Are you flirting?'

'That's not the right question. The question should be, whether you're liking it or not.'

'A cigarette takes about two minutes to start affecting your liver. And you took less than *that* to touch my heart with your flirting skills...'

Shaurya didn't say anything. Sensing the awkward silence, she said, 'I'm sorry if I have offended you.'

'No, not at all! It's just that the last time someone gave the two-minute reference, it was very insulting,' Shaurya said.

The girl looked confused, but still smiled.

'Nevermind! By the way, here is your Davidoff.' She offered him a cigarette and he realized that her blue eyes were more toxic than the cigarette itself.

'Thanks! Cheers to our first cigarette together,' he said. They cheered it like a fine glass of wine. As they took their first puff together, they smiled.

'So, if I need to meet you again someday soon, you'll be available here, selling cigarettes?' Shaurya asked and she laughed.

'I like your sense of humour already. I am not lucky enough to be selling cigarettes here. You need to find me elsewhere.'

'I would like to know where, because I like returning favours. And soon.'

'Aren't you too quick?' she said.

Her words again reminded him of what Mehr had said while breaking up. Even though the reference here was different, but a part of him got stuck to the word "quick".

'Well, I kind of am. I don't like to waste time,' he spoke.

'Well, if you live anywhere nearby, I think I'll see you around.'

'Oh, have you shifted here recently? Because I haven't seen you here earlier.'

'I've just shifted a while back,' the girl said.

'Where?'

'There!' she said and signalled towards 'Prayas'.

'What a joke! That is the newly-opened correction centre. Only bloody prisoners and murderers live there,' Shaurya said and laughed it off.

'Yes! I am one of those.' After taking an obvious pause, she said with sincerity in her voice.

'You've got a nice sense of humour,' Shaurya said. She didn't look impressed and that changed his expressions.

'You can give me the half-used cigarette if you don't like taking it from prisoners,' she said, sounding dead serious.

'Oh, I am sorry. I mean, I've never come across a prisoner in my life, so I don't know how to speak to one,' he said and realized that he had ruined it even more.

'No worries! You wouldn't get many chances to speak to one in the future too. It was nice smoking with you,' she said and disappeared from there, in a jiffy.

Shaurya tried stopping her, but he neither had a reason nor had a name to call out to her.

He had just encountered the first prisoner on the street and she wasn't as cruel as he thought prisoners would be. He wanted this conversation to go on for long, but he also knew that he had lost a golden opportunity.

The cigarette vendor looked at him and spoke, '*Aapka toh pehli baar mein hi kat gaya bhaiya. Bina cigarette ke dhua dhua ho gaye aap toh.*'

Shaurya looked at him and decided to just move on from there without saying anything. As he walked towards his home, he thought about the crime she would've committed to reach here.

For the very first time in his life, Shaurya understood that looks can be deceptive.

7
Second Chance in Love

Roshan was watching news at home. Every time an anchor shouted, he changed the channel. He had been changing channels for the last half an hour or so, finally stopping at Rajat Sharma's news broadcast. Unlike others, he never shouted. He delivered the worst news in a calm and composed manner.

Sitting idle on the couch with a thermometer in his mouth, he was waiting for the thermometer beep to confirm his body temperature. It was 100.7 degrees.

He put aside the thermometer, but then picked up another one to check temperature afresh. To be doubly sure. Alongside, he kept checking the temperature of his neck and ears using the back of his hand. After a minute, the thermometer beeped, showing 100.7 degrees.

He hated being sick. Not because it confined him to home, but because he never had anyone to pamper him. He had lost his parents when he was young, and his wife always asked him to keep doing something or the other when he was sick. Her logic was that it would help him divert his mind. He didn't know how it felt to be pampered. Maybe that is why he kept pampering strangers in so many ways. He also tried to pamper himself sometimes. He'd call a masseuse, who'd give him a good head massage and kept talking to him for hours and hours. At other times, he'd just visit an old friend and talk to him about how cool it was being a kid. But today, it was too late to call a masseuse and he didn't feel like going out to meet a friend.

He took a Paracetamol and kept the stuff aside. He gathered some energy and walked up to the terrace. Maybe fresh air could do him some good!

He was lost in thoughts, when his phone beeped with a notification:

> *Age is no bar anymore to find love in your life, Roshan. Get loved 85 times at the age of 85 years.*

He felt disgusted at the notification he had just received. He looked around to see if Shaurya was there. He wanted to scold Shaurya for installing this ridiculous application on his mobile. Roshan came from a time where loving wasn't just about swiping it right or left. It was about looking at a person for once and then saying a yes or no to it. Well, it still wasn't very different. What used to happen in person back then was happening on mobile now. Right swipe for a yes and left swipe for a no.

When he couldn't see Shaurya anywhere, he hesitantly convinced himself to open the application named "Binge Date".

He clicked on it, and a fancy app screen flashed in front of him. It screamed bright colours and redirected him to the personal profile page. It was so user friendly that it kept suggesting things to be done – filling in name, other details, uploading pictures, creating a bio line that suited Roshan's interest. It even picked Roshan's birth date automatically, and suggested a line – "85 years young" or "85 summers experienced". Roshan chose the former and smiled.

Finally, it asked Roshan to choose between either the filtered picture or his real picture, which captured his warm personality. He chose the real one. Within ten minutes, Roshan's profile was complete! He was asked to start finding the true love of his life by exploring other profiles and showing interest.

Roshan was casually checking the app and learning on his own. He was liking the technological ease of it. He came across a profile that said, 'Stop living in the past; start living in the present.' It reminded him of his deceased wife and he suddenly wanted to know this woman a little more. That dimple, that side profile, the kind of clothes she wore and her smile quite matched that of Neeru's. As he saw the pictures of this 70-year-old woman, he couldn't help but send her a match request by swiping.

It looked like he was looking for a match, but only he knew that he was looking at a chance of getting closer to a person who remotely looked like Neeru.

He knew that Neeru wasn't going to come back, but when you need something desperately, even a strong illusion does the job. That's what happens when you lose a person – you start finding that person in the smallest of the things around. Sometimes some words would remind you of that person, sometimes a smile, sometimes a fragrance and sometimes, just your favourite song!

Roshan was amazed at the similarities between Neeru and this woman named Zainab. He convinced himself that if Neeru was alive today, she'd look almost similar to Zainab. He kept looking at her profile.

Zainab, according to her profile, was a separated mother, wife and daughter. No matter how dangerous it sounded to Roshan, it surely attracted him. It was the first time in the last sixty years that he had thought of taking another chance in love. Just like an impatient kid, he started waiting for her to match his profile so that they could chat.

He got a match request from a young girl who wrote, '*Uncle, ja ke apni kabr ki booking karo!*'

Another one said, '*If we date, what should I call you? Dadaji or Par-dadaji?*'

He realized that they were the ones whom he had ended up sending the match request to. Zainab, whom he wanted to actually connect with, he had swiped left and rejected.

He cursed himself for unknowingly rejecting her. He opened a picture of Neeru and in his mind, started comparing her with Zainab.

He wanted to find a way to fix it, but his phone battery died. Roshan realized that getting love in this life was getting next to impossible for him. As he dozed off that night, he silently apologized to Neeru for even thinking about another woman.

8
The Hug

Shaurya was trying to get some sleep. He kept switching the air conditioner on and off. He kept adjusting the blanket and tossing in bed, but sleep evaded him. He finally gave up. He sat up, took a bath and kept thinking about all those times when he had made love to Mehr. It was bothering him that she had never complained about this before.

As he came out of the bathroom, he picked up his mobile phone and Googled 'How to last long in bed'. It showed various methods to do so. One of it asked to use condoms, another one asked to learn the pause-squeeze method, one advised to distract yourself. Shaurya thought, *What the fuck! If I distract myself while making out, how would it even make sense? It's like eating a chocolate sizzler but thinking about bitter gourd. Why would anyone do that?'*

He closed that window and searched again with a different keyword. That showed him some exercises that included planks, glute bridges, jump squats, Kegel's, push-ups and pigeon pose. It also referred a video.

It was 2 a.m. and he went to the terrace, exercising as directed by that video. That two-minute comment Mehr made had hurt him a lot. He realized that the last time he had exercised was when he and Mehr had joined a fitness club together and Mehr had asked him to foot all the bills.

Shaurya started exercising, and after a few initial hiccups, he plugged in his ear-pods and carried on. Aarav saw him from a distance and kept calling out to him, but Shaurya was lost in the music. In his fifth routine, a tennis ball hit Shaurya's right eye and as he turned towards his left, he found Aarav standing at his terrace.

'Hey, how are you doing?' Aarav called out from a distance.

'It was going just fine till this tennis ball hit my eye. I was wondering who the hell is up so late!' Shaurya said as he caressed his eyes.

Aarav jumped a few terraces to come closer to him. 'Oh, it looks bad,' Aarav said.

'Yes, thanks for acknowledging,' Shaurya said getting surprised at the audacity. 'A simple sorry or "oh it was my mistake" would make this situation a whole lot better.'

'Stop looking for an apology. I was calling your name for the last five minutes and you weren't event listening! What other option did I have?'

'The one you just opted for! Jumping down a couple of terraces and coming here?' Shaurya said sarcastically.

'I didn't know my throw was so perfect. It never hits the stumps when I play cricket,' Aarav said casually. 'Aren't you feeling cold?' he added, adjusting his jacket.

'People who exercise doesn't feel cold. Those who spoil their effort, definitely do.'

'Ah, forget it! By the way, why this last-minute preparation for the marathon tomorrow?'

'What marathon?'

'The one that starts from Bandra and goes till Colaba? The one supporting LGBTQ, transgender love and spreads the message of "Love knows no boundaries"!'

'And why would I participate in that marathon?'

'I don't know, I just thought that you're exercising at 2 in the night, you're probably prepping up for the same,' Aarav said as he sipped the cold drink from his bottle.

'Are *you* participating in it?' Shaurya asked as he raised his eyebrows.

'Yes, I am.'

'Then why aren't you exercising?'

'Because I am not there to win, I am just there to spread the message and support the thought behind it,' Aarav said. Shaurya was thoroughly confused by now.

'Oh, I didn't know that! I mean… Yes, of course you have all the right to love whoever you want to. I support you. I am around if you need to talk about it.' Shaurya looked anxious and shocked as he assumed that Aarav is gay.

'I am not gay. Relax!' Aarav said.

'Oh ok, but even if you were, I would've been there to support you,' Shaurya said and tried to sound as normal as possible.

'Are you okay, Shaurya? You seem to be a little lost. You are exercising at the weirdest hour! Your muscles could come out and scream for disturbing them so late in the night,' Aarav said and Shaurya took Aarav's bottle to sip the cold drink. That's when Shaurya realized that there was alcohol mixed in the cold drink.

'Why are you putting cheap alcohol in cold drinks? Your father has the best drinks collection in the entire town!'

'Exactly! That's my father's. Not mine. He wouldn't let me touch a drop of it. My father is rich and all, but I am still poor. Cheers to this!' Aarav said in a very 'I don't give a fuck' way.

'How's your equation with your father?' Shaurya was curious now.

'We greet each other when we get up in the morning and we wish each other a good night.'

'What about lunch and dinner?'

'I don't remember when we dined together last. His days are for his work and his nights are for new dreams about work.'

'You don't feel like spending time together?' Shaurya said as he casually checked the last seen of Mehr on his phone. That's what he did daily, matching it with the guys with whom she might be going around. That was the main reason behind him getting sleepless nights. He was still busy with his mobile.

'I used to, but now, I don't feel like it anymore. I don't like talking to people who look at their mobile phones, pretending to talk to you,' Aarav said.

'Oh, I am sorry. I was just checking something important,' Shaurya apologized hastily.

'I wasn't talking about you; I was talking about my father. He's as fake as his social media account. He pretends to be happy, but he's not,' Aarav clarified.

'That's strange!'

'Not really. I am used to it now. He doesn't exist in my life anymore.'

'Don't say that! He's still your father.'

'Your definition of parents and mine differs. My parents died well before your parents passed away. The only difference is, I can still see them.'

'Well... that's deep. You are quite mature for your age.'

'Thank my parents for it. My family's image is that of glass and they're scared it'll break. So all of us, rather than enjoying our lives, are just worried about the glass that *might* break down someday,' Aarav said. Shaurya just nodded in a yes.

Aarav finished the last sip of his cold drink and started walking towards his home.

'And by the way, doing those exercises helps your duration in bed when you do it in the *morning*, not late at night,' Aarav said.

'How do you know?' Shaurya sounded surprised.

'I've tried exploring my life a few days back and we probably landed up on same Google link, Shaurya.' Aarav smiled. 'See you tomorrow morning. Let's go to that marathon, if you wish.'

Shaurya started doing his exercise once again, but couldn't continue. He checked Mehr's last seen once again and noticed that she was still online. Reason enough for another sleepless night!

That's what happens when one of you moves on in a relationship, and the other one still stays where you've left him/her. Mehr was already miles away from the relationship and Shaurya was yet to make a move.

9

Life is a Marathon!

The morning didn't feel like other Mumbai mornings. The news channels were busy reporting that this was the coldest Mumbai had ever seen in the last twenty-five years. It was 20 degrees Celsius during day time and 9 degrees during late night hours. But the energy with which the news channels reported made it sound like Mumbai was under heavy snowfall. One enthusiastic journalist reported it standing atop one of the tallest skyscrapers in Mumbai. He confidently stated that people could only hear the sound of wind and nothing else. He was continuously talking about how difficult it was to stand there and report this live from Mumbai. He sounded like a person who had just gotten a better increment and promotion than he had ever expected.

Shaurya had somehow slept well after those exercises, the physical fatigue overtaking the mental chaos. His average sleep of eight hours had anyway dropped to three hours a night. His sleep was disturbed by a bad dream of his grandfather passing away. He rushed to see if Roshan was fine and was relieved to see him sleeping peacefully.

It was 5:45 a.m. Just then, his phone tinkled with Aarav's message. *Hey man! You up? I am going for the marathon. Like to join?*

Have no other choice. A bad dream spoilt my sleep. Be there in 10 minutes, Shaurya typed back as he put on his jogging tracks.

Soon enough, Aarav and Shaurya reached the starting point of the marathon – Bandra Worli Sea link. They saw hundreds of people flaunting the marathon T-shirts, taking selfies and making vlogs. They saw some old-age TV and film actors waiting to be recognized and taken a selfie with. But Mumbaikars don't pay much attention to actors, until it's a very big name.

There were some left-wing supporters praising the cause of the marathon and a few failed politicians trying to harp on the cause by extending their support.

Aarav arranged for the T-shirts for both of them and they started running. Some people were hideously dressed to show their support for the LGBTQ community. Shaurya also saw transgenders narrating the struggle stories of their life and an old transgender named Sehar telling everyone the advantages of being a transgender in a stand-up piece.

People who were running also took a moment to hear what Sehar had to say. 'We transgenders are the most privileged; we don't have to choose which toilet to go to! Both the options are open for us.' Everyone laughed.

'All the talented people need us the most, because when your colleagues don't clap, we still do,' Sehar said and everyone started laughing. That laughter was somehow key to the acceptance towards this community.

People were amazed at a transgender speaking like this for the very first time. Shaurya and Aarav had never heard his name and he didn't even look like a stand-up comic, but whatever he said there won many hearts.

Shaurya and Aarav kept running and saw Rahil and Rishabh Malhotra, the two big TV faces in India, also there. Shaurya spotted them.

'Hi Rahil bhaiya! What brings you here?'

'My PR agency asked me to participate in these social activities, so I am here. Things you have to do when you're a public figure!' Rahil said, noticing Aarav.

'So, both of you...?' Rahil half asked his question, suspecting them to be a couple.

'Firstly, we're not gay. And secondly, even if I was, my choice would've been better,' Shaurya said and Aarav looked at him. Shaurya started running faster, laughing out loud.

'I think he saw a better option,' Aarav said and started running behind Shaurya.

Shaurya was running so fast, as if he would win it all. Just when he had covered barely a hundred metres, he slowed down. He had spotted Mehr, kissing a top-notch female designer, Ruchi Walia. Shaurya was shocked.

Both the girls got into a Mercedes and suddenly, everything started making sense to him. He was just confused between two things – Was Mehr a lesbian all this while, or was she so hungry for money that she had decided to change her sexual preference?

He felt a little relieved that she hadn't ditched him for another guy, but still felt bad that she was no longer with him.

At that moment, Shaurya felt that life is just like a marathon. It has a starting point and it has a finishing point. You'd keep meeting different people in the journey, you'd meet some people you wouldn't have expected to make you laugh, you'll meet someone after a long time, once a best friend, who'll act as a stranger. Then maybe you'd meet someone whom you trusted the most, whom you think you knew the most, who suddenly turns out to be a completely different person.

But then, you tell yourself, that this life is a marathon and you have all the chances of not finishing it in top three! But when you'd reach the finishing point, you'd expect a smile to grace your face.

10

Roshan woke up a little late. He checked the time in his forty-year-old alarm clock and it showed 8 a.m. He would generally be up by 6:30 and go for a walk with Lakhan's father and a couple of more people. But as winters arrived; everyone packed themselves in blankets. No one had showed up for morning walks in the last few weeks.

He picked up his mobile phone from the side table. The first thing he saw was a list of notifications from girls calling him "*tharki buddha*" and what not! Then, he received a new message that opened his eyes.

Hi papa,

It's been long since we spoke. I miss you and the times that we've spent together. I also regret that I can't do it now. You know it better than anyone about how life has changed in the last few days. I am so sorry for what happened that day. I regret my words and nothing in this world can do anything to ease my guilt.

If it was like the normal times, I would've personally come to wish you on your happy birthday.

But you know, how things have changed. It looks difficult right now. But here's wishing you a very happy birthday. I hope you'll reply to my message today because I miss talking to you.

Lots of love,
Your son

Roshan kept reading and re-reading the message in utter surprise. He didn't know how to respond. This message surely left him speechless. Even before he could realize it, a tear from his eyes rolled down his cheeks. This moment made him all the more vulnerable. This message reminded him of something painful. From his eyes, it was evident that he missed his son badly. This made him remember the worst night of his life.

ᘓ

That Night

On Soham's birthday, after spending some time with Lakhan and his wife Sia, Soham and Smita were heading back home. It was a very long night for both of them as just before this, they had celebrated Soham's father's birthday. No matter how much Lakhan and Sia insisted, they didn't drink because they were supposed to go on a long drive.

It was 1:30 a.m. and Soham was feeling very sleepy.

'Let's go for a quick drive?' Smita asked, more like a request.

'Like this? I am already in my dreams,' Soham said, struggling to open his eyes.

'That you always are, even when you're awake. So, don't worry! One quick drive wouldn't be a big deal! You're always busy with your work anyway,' Smita insisted.

'If you insist, let me ask papa as well,' he replied.

'No yaar, not tonight! You both would start discussing his love for old things and I would get bored.'

'Okay, let's go!'

She asked, 'Don't you think we should at least tell him that we are going to be late?'

'You know if we interrupt his sleep, he would be awake the entire night,' Soham wasn't sure.

'But you also know that if he gets up in the middle of the night and he is unable to find either of us, he'll get worried,' she said and he agreed.

'Okay, let's just quickly tell him that we'll be back in an hour or so,' he said. As they carefully entered the house and went closer to the old man, he hugged them both in sleep.

'You're still awake?'

'How can I sleep when my kids aren't back home?' Roshan said with a smile on his face. His eyes were beaming with love and care.

'That means that either we would never get a chance to go on long drives during the night or you would never get a chance to sleep when we're out.'

'Don't worry! You hardly get free time for each other. You both work crazy hours! Just go on a quick drive and come back safely,' he said as he hugged both of them tighter.

They both started walking outside. Suddenly, Soham felt a strange urge to hug his father one more time. As he hugged him, he had tears of love in his eyes, which left Roshan surprised. Before he could ask anything, Soham said, 'Happy birthday once again, papa. I am taking your watch with me. Will come back soon.'

Soham and Smita started walking towards the door.

'Come soon, I'll sleep peacefully after that!'

What came next was a phone call from an officer on duty. Just like everyone, late-night calls scared Roshan as well.

'Is it your car? MH 04, AA, 9898?' the officer asked.

The next few minutes turned out to be the toughest few minutes of his life. He kept crying as he knew what he was about to see next. He knew that his birthday had brought the worst news of his life. He knew that no matter what, he would never be able to undo what had happened.

He kept slapping himself harder and harder and felt guilty for not stopping them from going out so late. When he reached the location, he opened the door of his car with shaky legs. With a tremble in his voice, he started crying. There was blood everywhere near the car crash.

His son, with whom he used to share everything, had breathed his last a while ago. His son, who hugged him twice before going for his last drive, was declared dead on the spot, along with his wife. They were soaked in blood. It was very difficult to identify them. The watch, which Soham had borrowed from his father, was soaked in blood. But even after his death, he was holding it tightly in his hand.

Soham and Smita had died exactly like they had lived – holding each other's hand.

That's life! It breaks you when you are least expecting it. It gives you the heartbreak and leaves you alone to heal.

The world would say time heals everything. The close family members would say that we're always there for you.

And then, someone would say, Soham and Smita are watching you from above. They always wanted you to be happy.

The ultimate truth is – when you have lost someone who was your life, how can one expect to live? And you know, what's worse? When you know that you have to live for others, in spite of how shattered you are!

And many people don't see it clearly, but you know what's worse than dying yourself? Seeing someone you lived for, die in front of your eyes.

Shaurya was expecting to see his parents and Dadu in the morning, so Roshan knew that he had to be strong and resilient.

From that night onwards, one thing that remained constant was – Roshan could never sleep peacefully during the night, as if he was still waiting for his kids to come back home safely, only hoping that if they'd hug him this time, he wouldn't let them go out of his sight.

11
The Ray of Hope

The next day started with even colder winds. Shaurya's sleep got disturbed as he received a call from a random person.

He never switched off his mobile while sleeping. He had heard traumatic stories of people who lost their loved ones to suicide and they regretted not picking up their call for one last time. Not that anyone he knew was showing signs of depression, but the mere thought of losing anyone close to him often jolted him. He would generally wake up at 6:30, but 5:30 still was a little too early for him.

Now that he was awake, he got up and looked around. The world was sleeping. He picked up a packet of bread and went towards the society pond to feed the beautiful fishes. He had been doing that for a long time, and loved it.

Shaurya was the first to enter the pond area at this hour. To his surprise, there was someone else on the other side of the pond, sitting with a loaf of bread. When he looked closely, he was happily surprised to see the same girl from Prayas who had offered him cigarettes that day.

Shaurya got up and started moving towards her. Just as they made eye contact, she said. 'You would probably want to stay away from a criminal, right?' It seemed she was still angry with Shaurya for making such insensitive remarks that day. And why shouldn't she be!

Shaurya preferred to remain quiet. He just sat a few feet away from that girl. She was taken aback by his silence. None of them spoke for the next few minutes. All they could hear were the sound of fishes munching the bread and the flowing water.

'You didn't answer me?' she asked him.

'Because I don't have an answer,' he replied

'A lot of people don't have answers to many questions that life throws at them,' she said.

'I agree.'

'You have a villa in one of the best areas in Mumbai. You are living with your parents who are rich and supportive. You would surely be the last person to know about life's difficult questions,' she spoke in a tone of obvious miff.

He kept quiet and waited for fish to finish the bread. As he got up, he replied, 'I lost my parents ten years ago in a fatal accident that was unfair. They just wanted to go on a drive to spend some quality time together. From that day, I've cursed myself daily for sleeping early that night. Either I would've stopped them or I would've joined them. My situation is the worst right now. I have an eighty-five-year-old grandfather who is my only family left. After him, I have absolutely no one to live this life with.

'So, you might be right! I am surely the last person to know about life's challenging questions,' he said it all in one go, with a satirical smile on his face. No matter how much he tried, he could not conceal his pain.

'I am sorry. I didn't know that. I mean, I probably judged you from what you said that day. I would be honest...

whatever I said just now is a reaction to the nasty things you said to me that day. I don't know how to apologize.'

'No worries! I am not going to cross paths with you, so you don't have to be so agitated. It was nice feeding fishes here,' he said in exactly the same tone as the girl had spoken to him that day.

'You're not the one who forgets easily, right?' she said and smiled.

'How do you know that?'

'I remember the "two minutes" thing from our last discussion.' As she spoke, Shaurya looked visibly uncomfortable.

'What a beautiful start to this morning! Thanks for bringing it up,' he said with a fake smile on his face.

When he was about to start walking, she said, 'So, it's 1-1! You made a mistake once and I did too. Both unknowingly!'

'I'm glad that you made a mistake then. Otherwise, you wouldn't have known the guilt I was living with all these days.'

'Trust me, I do. If there's one thing that I've ever learned, it's living through guilt. The worst part is, it never gets easier. It keeps eating you from within,' she said with conviction.

Shaurya kept listening to her intently. He wanted to ask many things, but he preferred to stay silent, as he did not want to offend her.

They kept walking and talking along the pond edge, appreciating the beauty around. Shaurya was looking more relieved and relaxed than ever.

'How do we live with the guilt then?' he asked.

'Well, things get easier if we know the consequences of our actions. If we convince ourselves that what we had done was the *only* option that was available to us. That did not have the luxury of choice.'

'Is it easy to convince ourselves?'

'If it was easy, we wouldn't have been discussing this right now. Nobody talks about easy things; they don't make stories. We all love delving into complex things because that's what makes a...'

'Story!' Shaurya completed her sentence. 'You're talking deep and it's all making sense.'

'That's what prison does to you. It makes you introspect. I spent seven years of my life there. I forgot how my regular life used to be. It's not easy to bounce back after you've spent almost a decade in prison, living between actual criminals and people like me.'

'People like you?'

'People who had no other option but to commit the crime. Our country's judicial system always talks about the crime, but no one discusses the intent and the reason. I wish there was a law which could dive deeper into the humane side as well!' As she said this, the first ray of the sun touched her face.

'What keeps you going?' he asked.

'It's this ray of hope.' She touched her face that was all covered with sunshine.

'Well, I assume that your morning hasn't started on such a bad note after all,' she said with a smile on her face.

'Not at all! It's been one of the best starts. But conversations become more interesting when we know the names of the people we're talking to,' he replied and smiled.

'Trisha.'

'Shaurya.'

They both introduced themselves with a handshake. But their endearing smiles were clearly the winning strokes this morning.

'Now, this is what I should call as a beautiful start to the morning.'

'Or a beautiful end to the day?' Trisha said, but Shaurya failed to understand what she meant by it.

'Why would you say that?'

'Because your day is my night and my night is your day. I wake up when the world sleeps and I sleep when the world wakes up. If there's one thing that you learn while living in a prison, it's to stay up the entire night to save yourselves from the monsters there.'

'So, is it some medical condition now?' Shaurya asked, trying his best to not sound stupid like the last time.

'Yes, Narcolepsy.'

'Oh! So what's your schedule like?'

'I sleep by 7-8 in the morning, so I still get to enjoy night walks, i.e., morning walks for other normal people like you. I get up by 6-7 in the evening, I get ready by 9-10 p.m. and then I have the entire night where I talk to myself, reply to myself, fight with myself and then cuddle myself if I am feeling low.'

'Oh, I heard about a UFO getting spotted a few days back! Did you step out of it?'

Shaurya asked as he smiled. Trisha laughed. 'That was a good joke.'

'I was nervous about cracking that joke. I didn't want to upset you once again. Well, how does this entire medical condition affect your life? Can this be resolved?'

'Doctors said that it can't be resolved as it is a part of my system now. Narcolepsy has changed my life by and large. I don't like crowded places; it suffocates me. I don't like people talking continuously. I hate long phone conversations and I hate public transport. The world might be full of billions, but I still prefer staying alone.'

'That's interesting! I mean, that's different and something that I've never heard of. I mean, it's...' Shaurya said eating his own words.

'It's complicated, but I've lived almost a decade of my life with this now, so I've kind of accepted this Narcolepsy as a part of who I am. It doesn't bother me anymore. Anyway, what do you want when this world keeps running? Peace! It's like a blessing in disguise for me. While the world is searching for it, I already have it,' Trisha said.

'So, good morning to me and a very good night to you. As the night comes, I too will have a good sleep I guess,' Shaurya said.

'Why so?'

'I always sleep better when I kind of clear things I have been feeling guilty of,' Shaurya said and added, 'I hope you understand.'

'I do! I've been living with guilt for years, so I surely do understand,' Trisha said and got up to leave. Shaurya looked happy.

They both unlearnt the perceptions they had for certain sections of people that day and made it simple. But people living at Beverly Hills weren't easy to convince.

People had started coming out of their villas for an early morning jog by then and these new friends in town were the reason behind many raised eyebrows.

The two worlds were about to come together. They would need each other to be each other's sunshine, when the times got dark.

12
Reality Check

Lakhan was flexing his muscles on the terrace top while handling the bulls and bears of the market. He had been known for his expert advice ahead of the times, that usually helped people invest in the right direction. It had taken him less than twenty years to build a company that was one amongst the top twenty-five stock companies in India now. In the meantime, he had also bought ten sparkling apartments in Mumbai. Though he stayed where his heart belonged – Beverly Hills.

He always fancied having an open gym on the terrace because of the cool winds that would be flowing from all directions to give him comfort. What's better than an open space to channelize your fitness goals!

He had finally set up the open air gym a few months back, but he never actually used any equipments. Today seemed like a very different day, though. Not only did he start exercising on the treadmill, but also put on loud music. He was behaving like a boyfriend who gets insecure when his girl's best guy-friend walks in. In this case, maybe he wanted to pass on a message that 'this society has always belonged to us and not to the criminals like you'.

Not that his gesture made any impact, but he felt that he did his bit by doing so. He saw a few criminals taking a walk.

They waved at him with a smile on their faces, but he rejected their gesture as he kept exercising. That re-affirmed the idea that they were not welcome here.

Manav got into the car and his driver almost killed one of the members of the correction centre. He opened the window and cursed his brains out.

'Don't you fucking know how to walk on a footpath? When you live in an elite society like this, at least behave like you live here. This isn't some rotten piece of your prison cell where you'd walk the way you want.'

Manav rolled up the windows and asked his driver to move ahead. Two prisoners, Sangram and Rashid, the two fittest oldies, walked away.

Rashid asked Sangram. 'What did he say?'

'He was welcoming us with open arms. He asked us to let him know if we need anything,' Sangram said with a smile on his face.

'It surely looked like he offered some help,' Rashid said and both of them laughed loudly as Rashid continued walking with a limp in his legs.

'What do you think the society members must be thinking about us?' Sangram asked, as he rolled his hands up and back to energise his body.

'Didn't we get a glimpse of it right now?' Rashid replied, still making sure if he was walking exactly on the footpath.

'I don't blame them either. It's like they have spent all their lives to get a villa of their choice, miles away from any dirt in Mumbai. And as they were busy enjoying their lives, dirt starts following them and rents out a place just between their dream place,' Sangram replied matter-of-factly.

'After all these years of suffering, you're calling yourself and others dirt! I know that this world will always see us as criminals, but how about we trust each other for a little longer?' Rashid said as he signalled Sangram to take a walk in the park. They both went inside the park.

'I don't doubt ourselves. I am just stating the obvious. Do you think your old friends and relatives will welcome you the same way that they used to?' Sangram said and laughed it off.

'They might!' Rashid replied.

'Then why didn't they come and meet you in last ten years? Your own son didn't take the initiative to meet you even once! Just ask yourself – if not you, who would've been behind bars?' Sangram asked. The question brought a lot of discomfort on Rashid's face.

'Well, how conveniently you spoil all my mornings with a topic like this!'

'I just give you a reality check at times! Nothing else.'

'Yes, you keep reading Osho and Ravi Shankar all day. And then, you keep me away from hope and demoralize me. How ironic!'

'I keep you away from false hopes,' Sangram said.

'Hope is hope. Don't differentiate between it like people do between criminals and citizens,' Rashid said as he geared up to do some exercises. It was one of his routines that he never missed since he was put behind bars. He was always thankful for being in jail for one reason. His time in jail pushed him to exercise more. Sangram and Rashid had bonded over their exercise routine and eventually became best of buddies there.

As the residents of Beverly Hills saw these two people in the park, they started collecting their stuff, packing their bags and left the park premises within the next few minutes. Their expressions had one subtext in common, "You're trespassers. You aren't allowed here."

As Sangram and Rashid witnessed the discrimination and ill-treatment, which they'd faced hundreds of times before, they received a notification. It was a new message from Sridharan that read:

Hello people,

As we all are heading towards the New Year's Eve, what better than bringing together two different families by having a long-awaited get-together. Beverly Hills is known for love and warmth towards its new members.

So let's party at Community Hall, tomorrow, 9 p.m. sharp.

Cheers to new beginnings!

As they both read the message, they felt that it might not go well with the people living there. It took them less than a minute to figure out that they were right. Upon reading the message, the expression of people changed from disgust to anger to fear.

13
Feeling Stuck

On certain evenings like these, when the traffic was less and the mood was pleasant, Roshan did what he liked doing the most. He took a walk on his favourite route and tried remembering how much it had changed. He would even remember the names of the old shops that existed there.

His love for old things was real and strong. He always believed that older things and people had those stories to tell, that the world needed to hear. He wore glasses that he had bought forty years ago, his father's old watch and vintage clothes. He preferred wearing his son's clothes, but never washed them, so that the last smell of him didn't go away.

Roshan couldn't let go of the people he loved so much. It's the one thing that he hadn't learnt in eighty-five years of his life.

As he reached the new urban café, he was taken aback. He couldn't spot the fifty-year-old food joint "Narayans", where Roshan and Neeru came to eat the most. He walked anxiously to see if he had come to the wrong place. When he spotted a paan shop, he asked, 'There used to be a shop here called Narayans. Where did it go?'

'The shop has been closed for a month. They couldn't afford the rent here, so they had to vacate it,' he said and saw the disappointment in Roshan's eyes.

'Did he not return your money as well?' he added.

After a few seconds, Roshan said, 'I would've given them money had I known that he was going through tough times.'

That's exactly how he felt when the Regal theatre closed down last year. That's where he used to watch movies with Neeru. An old place closing down hit him as much as the death of his loved ones. These were the places that were a bridge between the present and the past memories that he had created with his wife. Seeing them getting closed one by one was disheartening for him.

As Roshan walked away from there, he kept remembering his wife. He reminisced how they often came here on their moped or sometimes, they would just walk, spending quality time with each other. He kept walking with his shoulders drooping and entered a narrow street. Then, he entered a lane where there was a lot of dump on the street and rats skittering.

Roshan kept walking till he reached a very old hut. It had cracks all over it, with overflowing drainage. It had a door that would just allow a dwarf to enter comfortably. Roshan got inside the door somehow and saw an old eunuch sitting and reading a book on a couch.

'How many times should I tell you to fix your door? Not many people who live here are of your size. Why don't you get it fixed? Roshan said as he opened the wardrobe and filled the most expensive wine in his glass. It seemed to be a ritual for him.

'I kept this door small so that visitors should bow down whenever they come and go,' Sehar said without taking eyes off from the book.

'You could use some courtesy to welcome your old friend rather than being so engrossed in your book,' Roshan said as he sat on the uncomfortable chair. 'You haven't even changed this old chair till now!'

'Like you, I also love old things so much that I don't want to change them,' Sehar said, still not looking up from the book.

'If you're planning to finish the book and not talk to me, I might as well leave,' Roshan said. Sehar didn't react.

'What the hell?' Roshan said with frustration, and finally Sehar dog-eared a page of the book and kept it aside.

'I like to finish one activity before moving to the next thing. I was just finishing a chapter. Welcome home!' Sehar said.

'Which book are you reading?'

'A book of a eunuch's dream that hopefully becomes a reality someday.'

'So you were reading a fictional story?'

'I was reading an aspirational story that will become a reality someday!' For the first time in a while, a smile flashed on Sehar's face. 'What brings you here after so many months?'

'Just got to know about Narayans shutting down. This is your area. You didn't even tell me?' Roshan looked visibly angry as he snacked on some peanuts.

'You already know the reason behind that, brother,' Sehar said, patting Roshan's back to comfort him.

'I want you to move on for good. You're probably the oldest man alive who still hasn't moved on,' Sehar said. Then, they both continued to play their half-played Jenga. Whenever they met, they continued the game from where they had left.

'You just said that you too have a thing for old things?' Roshan said as he removed a Jenga block successfully.

'I like old things, but I am not obsessed with them. All old things in this world have an expiration date, just like a human body. As soon as we accept this truth, we discover our way to move on. But, not able to accept new things has always been your problem... since school. Remember the first time when I told you that I am not like you. When I shared my secret that I was a eunuch, you didn't speak to me for two years! When everyone else got to know about my real identity, they stopped talking to me too,' Sehar said, removing a wooden block which shook the entire Jenga building.

'I was shocked. How many times do I have to explain this to you? I was a kid.'

'I was a kid too.'

'Why are we discussing it today? I came here to share that a part of my life is over and I feel really bad about it. You're just making it worse for me. I miss my wife. I deal with an immense void and sorrow every day. Now, I will start missing the places too where we created those priceless memories. What would my life be left with?'

'Your life will still be left with the present. It is the moment that's going to be your past someday, which you'll start missing once it's gone. Then, you will realize the importance of this moment.

'I sometimes feel like a man and then, sometimes I feel like a woman. If I stop living in the present, I'll confuse myself endlessly,' Sehar tried removing one of the two wooden blocks since he was not sure, but finally, he removed another one with confidence.

'If all these places that Neeru and I have in common keep getting closed, I'll have nothing left to live for. I feel stuck.'

'You'll still have Shaurya! Unlike me, who has nobody but myself to live for.'

'I think we'll always disagree on certain things.'

'We've always differed on many things. It's time that we agree on something, bhai.'

'That looks highly impossible as of now,' Roshan said. As he tried taking the most difficult of the wooden blocks out, the Jenga building collapsed on the ground.

'The game we were playing for one year has finally come to an end! Wouldn't you like to make a new start before your life crumbles like this?' Sehar asked Roshan, but he didn't look much interested.

'People jump off mountains if a eunuch asks them to do so! And here, just because a eunuch is your oldest friend, you don't pay heed to my advice! You'll soon realize it though,' Sehar added.

As Roshan got up, he received a notification from Binge Date that showed that a woman named Zainab had super-liked his profile. He was surprised to see that it was the same woman he had left-swiped by mistake a few days back. He felt like he was inching closer towards his Neeru. He told himself that he was not finding love; love was coming back to him. He knew that it was most definitely his Neeru who had planned it for him.

That brought a smile on his face. The disappointment of Narayans closing down faded a bit as his heart was filled with happiness. Love comes with a certain convenience. One of them is that love has no age!

Roshan decided to walk down to his home, no matter how long it took. He super-liked her profile back. That evening, he warmly smiled even at strangers, making a start towards cherishing the present moment.

14

It was 7:30 a.m. Neeru was sitting and taking in all the natural sunlight, as the doctor had advised. Roshan was doing his yoga. Neeru was keeping the count of it and Roshan was trying to skip numbers so that he could get over with this sooner. He just wanted to go, get a pastry for himself, that he'd been craving for since last night.

'You're skipping numbers, Roshan,' Neeru said. Roshan tried to guard his eyes from direct sunlight and said. 'You're just counting it slowly, and counting it wrong.'

'I have always been better at math, so you stop schooling me please. I know you're hurrying because you want to run to that Parsi pastry shop and fill yourself with calories.'

'Darling, I eat calories so that we can burn them together.' Roshan winked, hinting at getting cozy with his wife.

'Better idea is to not take excess calories,' Neeru said with a stern face.

'Why are you like that?' Roshan asked.

'Like what?'

'Like this? You never get romantic. Whenever I try to get closer to you, you just end the topic. Why do you always do that?'

Neeru said nothing for the next few minutes.

'It kind of hurts me sometimes. It's been decades…you doing that,' Roshan said

'I couldn't say it earlier, but I also regret not being close to you. I regret not cuddling you and I regret not doing enough things when I could. I wish I made more memories with you,' Neeru said with a visible regret on her face.

'Why don't you do it now?' He asked, hopeful. 'There's so much more that we can explore now.' Neeru kept looking at him with a fixed gaze. 'Why are you looking at me like that, Neeru?'

'What else do you expect me to do, Roshan? You're asking for the impossible,' she said and smiled in disbelief.

'Everything is possible if we wish to make it possible.'

'You can do everything, but can't get a dead person back in the world. It's been two decades that I've died and you need to get over me now, Roshan. It's time you move on! The world is calling you; you shouldn't ignore those signals.'

'How can I love someone when I loved only you for my entire life?'

'I am not alive now and for you to be alive, you need a person who keeps you alive. You spread happiness everywhere, you keep even strangers happy, but that would die someday if you're not happy from inside. All I am asking is for you to treat yourself with love. You might end up making even more people happy. You are the reason behind people's smile; now I want you to meet a person in real, who's going to be the reason behind *your* smile.'

'What should I do?'

'Meet Zainab! Make her feel special. Let go of the past. You already believe that she's like me. It's even better for you.

That way you'll love me and her, both. Don't stop yourself now. Ignore all the love-happens-only-once definitions. It's time for you to create your own definition of love, Roshan. That's how you'll be able to make me happy even after I am gone from this world.' As Neeru said this, Roshan saw her voice and her visuals fading away in front of his eyes. He tried holding her, but he couldn't, and with a pacing heartbeat, he opened his eyes to realize that it was merely a dream.

He sat up straight and kept questioning himself, 'Was this a dream that felt too real or reality that felt like a dream?'

He saw his and Neeru's happy picture just in front and believed that it was a signal from Neeru.

He felt less guilty now. He went back to bed. That night, Roshan and Shaurya slept well, both ridden of their guilt.

Also, both of them were on the brink of a new beginning. Come to think of it, nobody is a bigger trader than a new beginning. It comes and takes away in its wake, all past memories.

15
Day Boy, Night Girl

It was midnight. Shaurya searched for all the top dating sites on Google and installed them all, one after another. He already had a couple of them on his mobile. He kept swiping right for everyone. He looked desperate to be in a relationship.

And as he went back to check his social media handles, he received a notification on Twitter regarding a breaking news that stated – *Famous designer Ruchi Walia discloses she was cheated by Mehr, who was pretending to be a lesbian for enjoying her wealth*.

Shaurya looked confused, shocked and disgusted. He always knew that Mehr loved money, but it never appeared to him that she could go down to this level for her love of money.

He dialled a few numbers of their mutual friends and gossiped his heart out. After a point, when he started feeling disturbed with all the badmouthing, he picked his car keys and went for a drive.

As he moved outside Beverly Hills, he saw Trisha looking happy and energetic.

'Hi, good morning.' Shaurya said and Trisha smiled back.

'You see how infectious my company is! It's just been a few days and you're already becoming a night person.'

'I would have loved it the other way around, though, but never mind! Why are you walking alone so late in the night?'

'Because I am the only zombie I know. Other people like sleeping in the night,' Trisha said as she came closer to his car.

'I can give up a night's sleep for you, maybe. Anyway, I've heard something that's going to keep me up at night.'

'That sounds interesting. You know my granny always narrated a story to me, before I went to sleep. I have missed that terribly since her demise. I wouldn't really mind hearing a story from you,' she said and sat in the car next to Shaurya.

'This isn't any fiction story, Trisha.'

'I like real stories even more. Are you starting already or want me to warm you up with some gross jail stories?'

'Ok! This isn't a story, I just got to know that my ex isn't a lesbian.'

'How does that even make sense?' Trisha's face was clouded with confusion.

'She broke up with me and then I found her kissing a top notch designer during a pride marathon.'

'Wait! What were you doing at that marathon?'

'I was there with Aarav.'

'Oh ok! I didn't know that you two were….a thing!' she said, but Shaurya laughed it off.

'I am not gay. Aarav just asked me to join the marathon. How can you even think that I am gay.'

'You just talked about your ex who was a lesbian. Then you said that you were at this LGBTQ marathon! You also said you were there with another guy. What in this world would that make me think?' she said.

'Precisely why I am not a story-teller,' Shaurya chuckled. 'I don't understand the chronology in which the story should be narrated.'

'So where were we?' Trisha asked.

Shaurya summed up his confusion in words.

'You still feel for her?'

'No, I don't.'

'Don't lie! Does it still affect you?'

'I don't even want to see her face ever again.'

'That means it still affects you. I too don't want to see the face of a person ever in my life and I know it affects me.'

'Well, I've moved on, but I just want to ensure, once in a while, that she's not happy,' he said, making Trisha laugh.

'Why so?'

'I want her to realise that she could be happiest with me. I want her to know that nobody in this world, guy or a girl, could make her feel as special as I made her feel. If I need to be honest, I would really enjoy her suffering the repercussions of her poor decisions.'

'You sound like a criminal with a plan.'

'Yes! We're twinning that way. Two criminals loitering around in the night and discussing their dark desires,' Shaurya joked, but Trisha didn't look too pleased with it.

'I am sorry, I was just joking.'

'How easy it is to joke on criminals, right? I'll pass this one though,' Trisha said as she smiled.

'You need to stop being so sensitive towards it now. You'll officially be a part of society very soon and you need to take jokes in a better way. It'll help you get out of it faster.'

'I've seen comedians serving their term in jail for the jokes they cracked, and also comedians serving their term for the joke they never cracked. So people outside the prison are extra sensitive. And don't worry, I don't take jokes seriously,' Trisha said. 'So, would you take me out somewhere for food or we'll just keep talking in your car?'

'Oh, I am so sorry! I completely forgot that it's your breakfast time,' Shaurya said and started the car. 'How does it feel to be the only person awake in the night?'

'Bliss! Plus, Mumbaikars care for people like me, so some of them keep their restaurants and cafes open. I relate with Mumbai very much. Mumbai never sleeps, just like me. I guess it's a medical condition both of us share.'

'What else is common between you and this beautiful city?'

'We both are warm, especially for the people we love,' she said and smiled. 'What about you? You tell me about yourself?'

'I love my grandfather. I am trying to hook him up with someone of his age so that he starts spending some time on his own. Then he can get away from his crazy habits.'

'You're the first grandson I've met who is trying to fix up his grandfather. You talked about him being crazy! What does he do?'

'He jumps the red signal and plays an oldie card. He gets free cakes from bakery shops. He'll get into the locals and talk to strangers as if he's known them for years. He'll still get into the building and ring the doorbells to irritate people in the middle of the night. He'll purposely walk slowly where people are playing cricket, because he hates cricket and loves football. He's 80 plus, but a kid at heart.'

'Your grandfather sounds like fun. Make me meet him sometime,' she said, amused.

'You'll get addicted to him. He's different,' Shaurya said, yawning. Already feeling sleepy.

'Your bed is already calling you, human. If you want to take a U-turn and go back, I won't mind. My day has just started, I'll go elsewhere.'

'I'd rather sleep in your arms than go back to bed tonight,' Shaurya said and smiled

'Are you flirting with me?'

'No, I am just exploring another option to sleep. Come on, I know better ways to flirt,' Shaurya replied.

'Where are we going?'

'A place where there are cold waves, where the land ends and water starts, where a species meets another species, where the moonlight showers its beauty on water and where there's peace,' Shaurya said in a poetic way.

'You could've simply said the beach! Why being so poetic?'

'*Jab shayri saath chal rahi ho toh andaaz shayrana apne aap ho jaata hai,*' Shaurya said and started doing 'Waah waah' on his own words. Trisha laughed. They both got down at one of the unexplored beaches of Mumbai.

They talked of Shaurya's childhood and how he missed his parents now. Shaurya talked about Beverly Hills and the people there.

Trisha kept talking about how everything in her life was going smoothly and suddenly everything had changed. They were speaking their hearts out for the very first time. It felt like they were a part of a different world.

Trisha realized that she had never spoken so much in the last ten years. At a certain point, she realized that she had forgotten so much goodness for some bad that had happened in her life. She remembered how she has visited this exact same beach with her family once. It brought all her memories back.

It felt like she was on the verge of crying, but if there's one thing that she had learnt in jail, it was to take control of emotions.

Shaurya was just being a good listener and as Trisha started to share her reason behind getting behind bars, she realized that Shaurya had slept in the middle of the conversation. It was the first time in ten years that she had dared to speak her heart out, and she still couldn't do it.

Trisha felt helpless and swallowed her words, like the hundreds of times before.

That's what happens when two different worlds meet. Not every night means glory for the night girl and not every day brings sunshine for the day boy. But still, their worlds intersect at some point daily. Now, all a night girl needed was the day boy to be her moonlight. A day boy wanted a night girl to be his shadow, that never leaves him.

16
New Year Celebration

We all get excited for New Year's celebration. We all expect the upcoming year to be better than the previous one, but does it always happen?

The lights and the decoration at Beverly Hills tonight indicated towards a hopeful beginning, but the expressions of the residents had a different story to tell.

This evening was all about fresh starts, but were the residents of Beverly Hills willing to accept and embrace the members of Prayas? It was a tough question!

The people, who often looked forward to such gatherings, weren't excited this time. Lakhan had lost millions today, Rahil's show dropped out of the top 10 TRP list for the first time since its launch and Manav lost a lucrative business deal. There were almost similar stories for everyone else too, but they were still more worried about their privacy and safety.

'This world will always find a reason to divide us. But I'll always find a reason to unite. I've tried to set an example that two different worlds can live peacefully with each other,' Sridharan said as he spoke with one of the prisoners staying in Prayas, while walking towards the community centre.

As he entered, he saw the residents of Beverly Hills sitting on luxurious sofas, and the members of Prayas sitting on a red cotton carpet on the floor. Pradeep Kanitkar had gathered all the residents in the community hall well before time so that he could execute his nasty plan of removing the sofas where the people of the correction centre were supposed to sit. It was his way of insulting them.

Sridharan was shocked to see this.

'The world, for you, must have changed drastically,' Sridharan commented.

'There is no doubt about that,' Manav said.

'I am not asking *you*. I am asking all my brothers and sisters from Prayas. So if you'd please excuse me?' Sridharan said as he removed his chair from the podium and sat on the floor, almost avoiding the residents. Everyone was surprised by this turn of events.

'Coming out of jail and successfully finishing your term without any red cards is an achievement in itself! All I can say is that you've definitely become more honest with yourself. However, it will take you some more time to get adjusted to the real world. This transition will enable you to bounce back stronger and lead a more meaningful life.'

'And what about the people who've been living their lives ethically? Is this a transition phase for all of us to become criminals?' Manav said. Everyone looked at him. Some of them felt disgusted while the influential residents of Beverly Hills supported him.

'I would like to agree with Manav. We're all respectable people living here. I don't understand whether it's a reward for these people or a punishment for all of us,' Lakhan said. He tried hard to conceal his anger, but failed miserably.

'How conveniently you've put all our lives in danger! Enough of our tolerance already?' Rahil said, which irked Sridharan.

'Coming from a chain-smoker who just smoked a joint outside, putting the lives of other people in danger is a joke! You all are forgetting that you live in Mumbai, where diverse people reside in every corner,' Sridharan said as he looked around to see everyone's expression. 'You are also forgetting that you're insulting a group of people on their faces who're saying nothing. If there's anyone who's tolerant enough here, it's these people and not you,' he added.

'What are we here for?' Sangram finally asked, unable to take the jibes anymore.

'We're here to introduce you to the Beverly Hills residents officially,' Sridharan said.

'So far, it's definitely not sounding like a meet and greet ceremony,' Sangram replied.

'Not everyone is like that, I am sure,' Trisha said. She looked around for Shaurya, but he was nowhere to be found.

'Just sharing cigarettes and feeding fish brought *that* change in you! That must be something powerful,' Sangram said whimsically.

'How elated I am to know that you're doing exactly what everyone does! You believe that we should not judge others and you seem to be doing the same thing?' Trisha replied. That surely raised some eyebrows within the group. 'Someone needs to bring a change.'

'It is ironic that criminals are talking about bringing a change. That's what the world has come to,' Rahil said. He laughed it off as he kept checking Instagram stories on his phone.

'Rahil, if you're here physically, then it's better that you are present here mentally as well, with all the possible manners that your parents never taught you. You're not a TV star here,' Sridharan said.

'And you're not the mayor of the city here, Mr Sridharan. You better watch your tongue before saying anything against my parents, alright? And stop sounding like a school teacher,' Rahil said. He looked intensely into Sridharan's eyes, much like his character from his TV show.

'I can school you too, if that's what you want. That's certainly something that you need. Your parents were so busy cheating on each other that they forgot to school their own kid,' Sridharan said. That made Rahil even more furious as he got up from the sofa and held Sridharan by his collar.

Everyone including Lakhan and Manav mediated. They didn't let this go any further. Rahil looked infuriated and kept yelling at the top of his voice. His body was shivering out of anger.

'Never ever in your life you'll say anything against my deceased parents. If you do it, trust me, I'll do what's required. Then I will be the one to go to this correction centre after thirteen years of imprisonment.'

Sridharan was indignant, but he chose to not say anything. He set his kurta in place, and just after a few seconds, put up a fake smile.

'If that's how you'd like to welcome the chief guest of the evening, I will graciously accept it. Time for some music and drinks, my friends. The floor is all yours,' he added and signalled the DJ to put some peppy music.

The DJ played some popular songs. The lights changed, but there was still no one on the dance floor. Manav and Lakhan, along with Pradeep, went to a corner to discuss important things. All the ladies went to the washroom to gossip. All the people from Prayas left as they didn't feel welcome. Sridharan also left for the evening.

Rahil was back to smoking cigarettes. Manav's young son Aarav asked for one as he didn't find his parents around.

Rahil asked, 'Are you sure?'

'More than ever!' He replied as he made sure that his dad wasn't around.

'Is it legal for you to smoke?' Rahil asked.

'Is it legal to spoil my childhood for politicians?' Aarav asked. Rahil didn't have an answer to it, so he offered him the cigarette.

'Here's to our first smoke together,' Aarav said and cheered with a cigarette

'We just know each other. We aren't friends.'

'You'll need one soon. All of us will. It's time to be thick with each other,' he said, trying to make rings out of the smoke. He almost succeeded at it.

'You know what? I also tried doing the same when I started smoking,' Rahil said with a smile on his face. 'I used to think that I'd look good while doing so.'

'When did you start smoking?'

'When I found out that both my parents were sleeping with somebody else's partner.'

'You must be quite young?'

'I was fourteen.'

'I started it last year. I was sixteen.'

'I had my reason. What's yours?'

'I started smoking because of FOMO, you know? Fear of missing out! Everyone around was smoking and I was the only one who hadn't tried it. I never had a good enough reason, to be frank, but now I got one. With this whole bunch of criminals loitering around our houses, I think of leaving India and settling abroad, maybe Canada.'

'Why Canada?'

'My long distance cousin lives there.'

'So?'

'I kind of love her. We are a thing when we are together. Our parents just don't know about it yet.'

'You'll be sent to the correction centre for a crime that you're going to commit.'

'Let it be! At least we'll stay together that way.'

'How can you fall in love with your own cousin, even if long distance? I mean that's like breaking a rule.'

'There are a lot of things people don't want you to do in love. And that's why they put all their reservations in a box and call it *rules*. Why do I follow what others feel when they don't follow what I feel?'

'I don't get your point.'

'Your parents surely must have understood,' Aarav said and wished that he hadn't. Rahil didn't see it coming. Aarav looked apologetic as he threw the remaining part of the cigarette and sprayed a mouth freshener to avoid any questions from his father.

'I was just being honest. I am sorry if I offended you in any way,' Aarav said and left without even expecting an answer from Rahil.

This was surely not the kind of New Year's Eve that everyone expected, with confused faces all over. But a few metres away, someone was smiling while chatting with a new buddy whom he had met on Binge Date. Roshan looked so delighted after years… or maybe, decades.

Trisha looked for Shaurya for one last time and when he was nowhere to be seen, she messaged him, *Where are you?*

He replied, *I slept till late in the day and had to be out for the new year's eve with a few friends.*

17
Kiss Luck

Shaurya was struggling to find a space to park his car. He kept going around in circles and finally found a place in about fifteen more minutes.

There are two things that annoy Mumbaikars – first, when they miss their local train and second, if someone snatches their car parking spot. That's exactly what happened with Shaurya.

But you know what irritates Mumbaikars more than anything else? When that *someone* who stole their parking spot turns out to be their ex's current boyfriend.

As soon as Shaurya opened the window to express his anger, he found Mehr walking out of the car. She was looking as slutty as ever. She was holding the hand of a guy who had a bigger car than Shaurya's. The worst part was that she hadn't even noticed him. Instead, she started making an Instagram reel with her boyfriend on a cheesy number which blocked the traffic.

Shaurya kept watching her stupidity from a distance. Then, he parked a little further, moved towards the elevator and pressed 42. Mehr, along with her new boyfriend Shaheen, got inside the elevator too.

That's where their eyes met. Shaurya and Mehr felt awkward. Since Mehr and Shaheen hadn't pressed any other floor button, Shaurya knew where they were headed.

With just the three of them in the elevator, Shaheen started kissing Mehr and she seemed to be enjoying it. A lot had changed since their last meeting. A Rolex watch and Louis Vuitton purse, to be precise. He suddenly remembered that she had never let him kiss her in the elevator, stating that it would spoil her make-up.

He tried his best to ignore them, but till when!

That's what happens with things that you try to ignore the most. You end up giving them more attention.

His mind remembered all those moments when he had kissed her and they had made love. He thought he was moving on and becoming stronger, but this sudden face-off had spoiled it all.

They came out of the elevators. Just after sharing a silly, "Oh baby, I love you more," they entered 4203 and hugged Sonakshi, the host of the party.

Sonakshi spotted Shaurya and invited him in.

He asked casually, 'How do you know Mehr?'

'I've known her for a while now. How do *you* know her?' she asked him, but the music was so loud that she repeated her question twice.

'I've not known her for almost two years.'

'What does that even mean?'

'That means that even after staying in a relationship with her for two years, I couldn't *know* her,' he replied.

As he walked inside, he saw the new couple in town getting cozy. The snobbish neighbours were making faces as they heard loud music.

'They must be doing drugs!'

After looking at all her fingers, Sonakshi chose to offer them the middle one.

It looked like one hell of a party, indeed. All the junkies from the town were present there. Some of them were completely stoned and the others were on their way to getting high. A guy who called himself 'Fakir' was narrating some verses from iconic poems. All of them were appreciating his performance.

Another guy, Advik was playing some melodious tunes on his guitar.

'This life isn't what you see, but it's how others perceive you,' Fakir said. The people who met him for the first time hailed him as the GOAT! Greatest of all times! The guy, with silver highlights in his hair and a red-coloured goatee, surely looked the most stoned, but also the most confident of all.

'You know what love is? Love isn't something that you do every day. It's something that you don't know, but still feel,' Fakir said the most random things. All the people there stood up in respect.

Shaurya felt out of place in this seemingly exciting party.

He saw a few strangers talking about creating a startup. The other stranger, whom no one was talking to, barged into the conversation and said, 'I can contribute fifty millions to start with.'

Their conversation ranged from *Khud ka kuch karna hai yaar* to *Forbes ka award winning speech mai likhunga* because I write well.

He saw an overworked employee attending a zoom meeting at this hour, convincing his boss that he was not partying.

A couple of people were discussing the likes of Black Sabbath, Slayer, Judas Priest and Led Zeppelin. As Shaurya filled a glass of scotch for himself and returned, he saw that they were making an Instagram reel on a Bhojpuri song. In this party, people were changing their musical preferences really quickly.

Mehr asked a bartender to make a Bloody Mary for her. As Shaurya noticed her around, he said 'Hey', as if he had just noticed her.

'Oh come on! Don't behave so formally. You could just be yourself.'

'So what the fuck are you doing here?' he said, almost venting out his anger which was suppressed within him for weeks.

'You were behaving better when you were being formal.'

'As if you were at your best behaviour when you said those nasty, insensitive things to me that day.'

'You still haven't moved on?' she said.

'No, but you moved on really quickly. From being straight to being a lesbian for money, and then from being a lesbian to going back to being straight once again – that too for money. You're quite a traveller, Mehr. Now I know why you never reached an orgasm with me. You probably needed dollars inside you and not what I had to offer,' Shaurya said it all at once. He felt relieved.

A couple of girls standing close by started laughing at Shaurya's words. The bar-tender handed Mehr a glass of Bloody Mary. Shaheen came and took her away for a dance.

'Start calling it Bloody Mehr,' Shaurya said to the bartender. The bartender just rolled his eyes and got busy with tossing the bottles to impress his customers.

Sonakshi, the party host, was looking gorgeous. The boys at the party tried getting their hands on her. Sonakshi and Shaurya knew each from the gym they both went to.

Through random conversations, they had become good friends. Sonakshi was the winner of the beauty pageant "Miss Maharashtra" and after failing to get a movie in Bollywood, she had started doing music videos.

Just then, the DJ played Sonakshi's popular song and everyone started chanting her name "Sonakshi, Sonakshi". After a few seconds of modesty, she jumped in and started dancing, which took the room temperature up a notch.

She was definitely the hottest one in the room. As she finished her dance, she did something that raised many eyebrows and gave many a boner. She started giving a lap dance to Fakir and then, they kissed and how! The lot cheered for the two.

Shaurya surely didn't expect this to come as a surprise. He was already overwhelmed by everything that was happening around him. He surely felt out of place. Not only because Sonakshi was his good friend, but also because she was hooking up with the most ridiculous person in the room. He ranked him the first on the list of fools, even though Shaheen and Mehr were around.

As they broke their magical kiss with Sonakshi's lipstick all over Fakir's face, he said, 'Love isn't about what you do when people are around. It's about what you do when you're alone.' With this, they stepped outside the room, lusting for each other.

'Keep yourself high guys, because you might not want to remember many things that happen here tonight,' Sonakshi winked and added. 'Let the lips meet when the clock strikes 12.'

After this official announcement, the couples started kissing each other. The only two persons who were left unkissed were Shaurya and the guy with the laptop. Their eyes met and for some reason, the workaholic guy started walking towards Shaurya. Shaurya signalled him to stay away.

What came after that was a surprise for many in the party. People randomly started swapping partners to kiss. As that happened, Shaheen, who looked the coolest amongst the lot, felt unhappy as Mehr started doing the rounds without thinking about how he would feel. They all called it "kiss luck" and announced that through this, they blessed each other with good luck.

Sonakshi and Fakir were making sounds louder than ever. The reels gang was still busy making videos and uploading them on Instagram. And the guys who were discussing the business proposals also started kissing each other.

Shaurya's ears ringed with the words that Sonakshi had said, *Keep yourself high guys, because you might not want to remember many things that happen here tonight.*

Suddenly, a few policemen, along with some special officers, entered the party. When they reached, everyone got scared as a lot of drugs were confiscated from the spot. All of them were put into the van. Some were naked while the rest of them were half-naked.

But one thing that was common for all – all of them were getting fucked tonight.

18
The First Date

At Beverly Hills, Roshan was chatting with Zainab, clueless about what was happening to his grandson.

'Let's skip all the pleasantries,' Zainab typed, which took Roshan by surprise.

'And jump to?' Roshan replied.

'Jump to why are we here?' Zainab texted.

'Isn't that too quick?'

'I don't think we have a lot of years left,' Zainab texted as she kept looking at her picture with her ex-husband and her kids. She was sitting on an open terrace, enjoying the view of the skyscrapers touching the sky. While the world was partying, they were lost in their conversation.

'That makes sense. However, I am looking at about a hundred plus years, minimum,' Roshan joked.

'You want to hike the mountains holding a stick?' Zainab asked.

'If only you'd be standing by my side.'

'Now I didn't mean you to be so quick.'

'I guess I took your age advice a little too seriously,' Roshan typed and Zainab smiled.

A part of their conversations always reminded him of Neeru. Every time he chatted with Zainab, he felt going closer to Neeru. Her matte lipstick, flawless skin and the confidence in her eyes made her much younger than her real age, exactly like Neeru.

'What do you do, apart from stalking oldies on Binge Date?' Zainab asked.

'I left swipe the profiles I like the most by mistake,' Roshan typed and Zainab laughed at this response.

'And when did that happen?'

'Few days before you super-liked my profile. I left swiped you by mistake.'

'And you remember the name as well whom you've left swiped? I wouldn't trust you if you say yes!' Zainab typed.

'I remember the first vehicle registration number I owned, all the phone numbers of my loved ones, the addresses of all the houses I changed and the bills of all the dates I've ever been to.'

'Must be a hard time for all your exes for whom you've bought gifts. You would be able to tell them how much you've spent during the relationship.'

'Or you can say how much I love cherishing the memories that I remember every detail of it.'

'I generally don't trust oldies, but that's all I get at this age! But you'd definitely have an interesting story to tell as you're trying to date at eighty-five.'

'Shouldn't be a very different story to tell than the woman who's trying to date at seventy.'

'One thing that never changes is that an old woman still has more options to date compared to an old man.'

'Talking about options, I always liked being a choice.'

'And you just impressed me for the second time in the last few minutes.'

'When was the first time I impressed you?'

'When you told me that you remembered everything about the past, even the minute details. People generally become forgetful at this age, but you are becoming smarter. That's impressive!'

'What about you? What kind of a person are you?'

'Mostly non-judgemental! I like being in the moment and not in the past. I like trying to reinvent myself and trying new things,' she typed.

'Like dating an old person in the seventies!' Zainab added with a smiling emoji.

'Age hasn't really mattered much in my life till now. I am sitting like a person in her forties and drinking what people generally drink in their twenties. I am enjoying my life thoroughly like people would in fifties. I guess that's enough to explain why I am a cocktail of all the ages I have lived. That is why age doesn't matter to me so much.'

'What brings you here?' Roshan was curious.

'My search for being loved. I always wanted to be loved in a way that satisfies my soul. I feel love should make you feel important. I wanted to be surprised in love.' Zainab got a little philosophical. 'Love surprises you less and shocks you more. That's my definition of love. What's your definition of love?

'For me, love doesn't have a standard definition. How can you capture something in words that is so evolving?' Roshan said as he received a message on his mobile. He was perplexed and emotional at the same time.

'How do you prefer calling a person? By her name or by a nick-name?'

'By a nick-name, if I am close to that person.'

'What's the nick-name you'd like to give me if we ever got close?' Zainab asked.

Roshan typed 'Neeru' and kept looking at the name as he remembered his wife. Roshan suddenly received a message on his mobile and he sent the message to Zainab mistakenly. He read the message he received on his number, which made him emotional once again.

Hi papa,

It's the beginning of a new year. A lot of people would like to forget what last year offered to them and might want to move on. That's what this world does. They sacrifice the past for the future, but I am still not up for it.

I wish it was as easy for me as it is for others. How can I celebrate the New Year till the time I haven't really moved on from the last few years? My idea of a perfect New Year was you taking us for long drives. Then, we would celebrate with some bonfire, music and a lot of family jokes.

I remember how you taught me to drive a car and how elated I was that day.

I wish I could speak with you once again, like old times. I wish I could be a better son at least for once. There's a list of wishes I have, which I know would never get fulfilled.

Life isn't the same without you, papa. I wish I could go back in time, but I know, it isn't going to be possible.

Wishing you a very happy New Year papa, wherever you are. I hope you get a better son in your next life.

I hope you reply to my message.

Lots of love,
Your son

Once Roshan read this message, there were tears in his eyes that failed to stop. He wanted to reply to this message, but something stopped him, like always. He didn't reply.

Zainab kept messaging. 'Is this your wife's name? Are you up, old man, or have you slept?' But Roshan didn't reply.

That New Year's Eve was unexpected for Roshan. Not because he chatted with Zainab on Binge Date, but because of what was coming next. Suddenly, he received a call from Sridharan.

19
Tough Times

'Happy New Year, Sri,' Roshan said as he picked up the call.

'I guess your TV isn't switched on right now,' Sridharan said as he picked up the call.

'I have stopped watching TV a long time ago. Even though the world is getting progressive, the TV content is becoming regressive.' Roshan stepped towards the television set and picked up the remote.

'The mentality of Beverly Hills is definitely not progressive. I don't think you know what happened there today.'

'Are they showing that drama on TV?' Roshan asked as he laughed it off and switched on the TV. He was flabbergasted when he saw Shaurya and the others getting arrested as they were caught partying with heavy illegal drugs.

Sridharan, who could hear the news on the phone, said, 'I just thought of letting you know. I know Shaurya is a nice kid. I don't think he was an active participant in this drug party. I called you to offer any help that you might need. That's the least I can do for my best friend's son.'

'Sri, I don't know what it is, but he's the only one I am left with,' Roshan said with shaking hands and a heavy breath. The man, who would find a reason to smile even in the darkest hours, was exasperated. The fear of losing his grandson made him restless. He had uncontrollable tears in his eyes.

'And I understand your situation. Let the investigation take place and we'll see what needs to be done after that,' Sridharan added.

'Investigation will be a little too late. What if…?' Roshan said and stopped his sentence midway.

'I would really suggest you to trust him more than you're doing right now. That's what he needs the most. There will be a lot of people who would pull him down. He needs someone to lift him up right now,' Sridharan said, sounding very concerned.

Roshan touched his chest to feel his rapid heartbeats. In that moment, he felt very old. He needed someone to hug him and say, 'Relax, I'll take care of it and get Shaurya out within no time.'

Though what Sridharan said was comforting, but it was more of an assurance than a promise.

'Would you come with me?' Roshan asked in a faint voice. He was literally begging him.

'I can't directly jump into it. It would just worsen Shaurya's stand in this entire scheme of things,' Sri said, and it made a lot of sense.

An eighty-five-year-old man, who was feeling young at heart just a while back, was feeling older than ever now. His shoulders drooped and his hopes started to vanish. But did he have any other choice? Could he just wait and watch? Was there any person he could turn to? Sadly, no!

♌

A car honked outside Roshan's house. Roshan's house bell got rung twice. When he opened the door, he found Sehar standing there.

'Not a great time to wish happy new year, Sehar.'

'I'm not here to wish you. I am just here to be with you. I thought you'd use a friend at this hour,' Sehar said. Roshan didn't say anything.

'Your friend has come all the way to meet you for the first time. Wouldn't you invite me inside?'

'Not a great time to be a host. I want to go and meet Shaurya right now,' Roshan said with red eyes. His eyes were brimming with tears which failed to stop.

'They will not let you meet him.'

'I can at least see him from a distance,' Roshan said in a hopeful tone.

'He isn't in some exhibition, Roshan. You need to stay calm and composed. You need to leave certain things, just the way they are,' Sehar tried to explain.

'It's coming from a person who doesn't have grandchildren? The person who doesn't even know the grief of losing a son!' Roshan said. Even though he realized that his remarks were insensitive, he didn't apologize.

'I may not have a dead son, but I had a family that considered me dead when the society got to know about who I really was. What more is needed to make a person feel disheartened when his eight decade old, thick friend keeps reminding him of how he is a eunuch first and a friend later?' Sehar said and got inside the house.

'I thought you'd leave after what I said,' Roshan said, looking deeply apologetic.

'I know exactly how it feels when someone, whom you need the most, leaves you,' Sehar replied.

'I'm sorry. I shouldn't have said those mean things.'

'You don't need to be sorry. Right now, you need my support more than I need your apologies.'

'I don't know what to do.'

'Face the reality! Wait for the investigation to get over. But more than that, be ready to face the storm of questions that would come your way. I'll pray for you and Shaurya,' Sehar said.

Suddenly, Sehar saw other people walking towards Roshan's house. He made way for all of them already. He knew that a lot of questions would be asked. He didn't want to be one of those questions that added to Roshan's worry.

Manav, Pradeep, Lakhan and the rest of the society members expressed their worry about Shaurya getting arrested. They all discussed it with Roshan and showed their confidence in Shaurya being innocent.

Manav said that they know Shaurya from his childhood. In no way, he could do something like this. Lakhan said that he trusted Shaurya more than his own kid. Pradeep said that he had seen Shaurya growing up and he was sure that he wasn't involved in drugs. They all offered sympathy and support to Roshan in this tough times.

That's what your loved ones do. They support you when you need it the most. They express confidence in you when you start losing it and they hug you when you feel lost and dispirited. If you've a neighbourhood like this, be happy that you live there.

But when you have people like Manav, Lakhan and Pradeep who showed support on Roshan's face but asked their kids to stay away from Shaurya, it's time you take a fresh look at your friends list, because when you count on them, they're mostly going to disappoint you.

The street, that was known for trust, love and brotherhood, has started to fall apart already. The united family of Beverly Hills was breaking up!

20
Hidden Truths

After three days of questioning, ADB (Anti-Drugs Bureau) got the reports. The last few days had been the most difficult for both Roshan and Shaurya. They were just allowed to speak with each other once on a call. Roshan's health deteriorated a bit as he was aware of the kind of rigorous grilling that Shaurya was going through.

After receiving the reports, the first one to get released from the police station was Shaurya. It was only possible due to Sridharan's consistent efforts to not drag him into controversy further, if he wasn't guilty. Some of them were given a bail and the rest of them were given a warning. There were news of settlements too.

After returning home, Shaurya became quieter than ever. He did not come out of his room for a week.

Roshan was surprised to see that all those people, who claimed to support Shaurya, didn't even come to see him once. It was only Rahil who checked on Shaurya every now and then. He made sure that Shaurya had someone to talk to. After three days in the police station and almost a week of isolation in his own home, it was the first time that Shaurya stepped out of his room. Roshan couldn't feel any happier on seeing him.

'What doesn't break you, makes you stronger,' Roshan said as he set up a bonfire on the terrace. He had searched for this quote on Google to make him feel more optimistic.

'You never really needed glasses Dadu, but this time you failed to see how broken I am. This motivational quote isn't really going to help me much,' Shaurya said, looking dull and sleepy. His eyes were looking more intense and red than before. He was trying to wear his jacket.

'There's a reason why I've put this bonfire. If you wear this jacket, the purpose of it being here will be lost,' Roshan said.

'What do you want to talk about, Dadu? About my drug habits? About how much of disgrace I've brought to this family? About how I am making your old days difficult?'

'Who told you I want to talk about any of these things with you? Forget about this, who told you that I want to discuss anything with you at all? I am just happy that you're back. I would burn weed to celebrate your home-coming, but that wouldn't be appropriate. And this time, I too might end up in jail. But there's someone else who wants to speak with you,' Roshan said.

Suddenly, Trisha entered and Roshan looked at Shaurya. She was wearing a black jacket and maroon lipstick. Her hair was neatly tied and her smile was brighter than ever. Shaurya definitely didn't expect any of this to happen.

'And talking about you making my old days difficult, I am still not old enough! Got it? I am using Binge Date and flirting with girls, much better than you've ever done.' Roshan's revelation left Shaurya more shocked than surprised.

'I was better off spending time in the police station than listening to your online dating stories. Too late, Dadu,' Shaurya said. Frankly, he didn't want this awkward conversation to get over because he was already feeling both nervous and excited. After everything that had happened with him in the past few days, he didn't know how to approach Trisha.

Roshan left and he played a soft little romantic tune in the background, winking at Shaurya from a distance. Shaurya kept asking him to stop the music, but he didn't listen.

'Your dadu sounds like fun.'

'He is!' Shaurya said and looked down.

After Roshan left, no one said anything for the next few seconds. Then, Shaurya took the lead.

'I'll be honest, I was thinking about how to start the conversation, but couldn't figure out the ways to do it.'

'How about starting it with Davidoff, the way we started our first conversation,' Trisha replied.

'It may not be such a nice idea to start a conversation with a person who just got back from the police station in a drugs case,' Shaurya said, trying to avoid an eye contact with Trisha.

'Come on! I know you have never even tried weed in your life. You're getting scared for nothing,' Trisha said with conviction as she put some more logs into the bonfire.

'How can you be so sure?' Shaurya asked, looking directly into her eyes for the first time.

'I've lived ten years behind bars. Name a drug and I'd tell you the best ways to do it. You name a drug and I'll give you ten more names.'

'I would rather speak to myself than play this drugs *antakshri* with you,' Shaurya said and she laughed. Her smile definitely lit up the evening. Shaurya kept thinking, how could a person look so relaxed and beautiful after spending ten years in jail! What could be her crime because of which she had to go behind bars?

'I am not offering you to play that. I am just telling you that spending time in jail can make you more mature than your age. That's what happened with me.'

'You did drugs there?'

'I was forced to take drugs. The kind of people and experiences you encounter within the prison walls compel you to take certain things that keep your guilt in check. You basically need something to not hate yourself every day.'

'So what happened with you there?'

'A lot of things that made me hate myself. When you have no one with whom you can share your feelings and perspectives, the right becomes wrong and the wrong becomes right very quickly. That's the thing with prison – You lose your wisdom within the first few weeks. Gradually, the reason behind why you were put there in the first place becomes irrelevant,' Trisha said, playing with a half burnt log. Other people might not like to touch it, but she looked quite comfortable while doing this. Finally, to his surprise, she broke the log and became silent.

'I never got to know about the reason why you were put behind bars.'

'But you've always wanted to know it, right?' she said. It seemed she had already sensed that this question would come her way eventually.

'No, not really,' Shaurya unconvincingly disagreed. He hated himself for lying.

'Don't lie! I catch it too quickly. And fair enough! People want to know the hidden, they want to explore the unexplored. That's where content lies. Knowing about something that no one does, already makes you feel better. Just like those people on their terraces who are watching both of us right now. They really want to know what's cooking between us,' Trisha said, pointing towards Manav Arora, who was standing with his younger son, Aarav, and Lakhan, who was standing there with his entire family. As Shaurya and Trisha turned to look at them, the Aroras and Lakhan's family looked uncomfortable at being caught red-handed.

'I just wanted to know it before because I was curious about the hidden. Now I want to know because I've been there and understand that world a little better. One thing is for sure, not everything that we see in prison is true. And, if we can't see something, it doesn't mean that it is non-existent. My perspective towards everything has changed dramatically.'

'What doesn't break you only makes you stronger.'

'My Dadu just told me that.'

'You agreed to it?'

'I didn't back then, but now that you're saying it too, I think I should.'

'That's what happens, we start believing the new people and don't pay heed to what old ones say. Precisely, why I was behind bars for ten years. I was very close to my step-father whom my mother married after separating from my father. My sister lived with my father and I moved in with my mother and step-father. I looked up to my step-father as he was the one who rescued my mother from a broken marriage, where she was humiliated every day. But I forgot to see the other side of the coin as my mother was equally to be blamed for the dysfunctional marriage,' Trisha said, with pain in her voice. Her hands were shivering, not out of cold, but due to her anger.

'My mother fell in love with her boss, who was divorced twice. He treated me like a daughter he never had. After some initial hesitation, I started calling him papa and it felt all good. I never trusted my sister when she said that he looked at her with lustful eyes. It's only after I found out that he had raped my sister for three long months that I realized that he was a monster. Once, I saw it once in front of my eyes. It was at that moment that I killed him mercilessly and I don't fucking regret it,' Trisha said. Her eyes were full of rage.

'If only I had trusted my sister, my sister wouldn't have faced this at all.'

There was a pause for the next few seconds. Shaurya kept looking at her to understand, how a girl like her could actually kill and live with it.

'What happened to your mother and the others in the family?'

'My father killed my mother for letting this happen to my sister. He's still serving his time in the prison. My real sister broke all ties with me.'

'Didn't she feel like meeting you even for once?'

'She did. She met me to say "thank you" but she also remained upset with me because she somehow felt that I was responsible for the fact that our father had to go to prison. She said that if I could understand her better, we wouldn't have lost both our parents. Since then, I never heard from her. I also tried going to the old house once, but she had left that place long ago. No one knows where she's now. Guess I am never going to know about her. I destroyed my family and I am the one to be blamed for this disaster,' Trisha said. Her voice mirrored the vacuum of her life.

'I am sure you'll see her someday.'

'It's not a movie, Shaurya, it's life! It's mostly ruthless. It's good to say that everything will be fine and you'll meet them, but then, that's fairy tale stuff and not reality.'

Shaurya had no answer to it. 'I don't know what to say.'

'It's still better than giving false hopes,' she said and smiled. 'Sometimes, you need a person who just listens to you and not say anything in return. That, in itself, is very reassuring. I wanted to speak about this that day as well, but you dozed off.'

'I am so sorry; I must have been tired.'

'No, no! I am sorry. I came here to cheer you up, not to scare or bore you with my life stories,' she said, realizing that she had spoken a little too much.

'You surely didn't do either of them. Suddenly, I feel that whatever I've been through is a lot less than the challenges that you have faced while you were in jail. I am glad to get some perspective on this. So, thanks for that.'

'You must be that sort of a person in your school who might feel bad that you nearly passed, but would feel much better if one of your friends failed,' she said. For the first time in the last ten days, Shaurya laughed heartily. Their amiable exchange became fodder for gossip between the neighbours.

♌

While taking a walk, Manav said to Lakhan, 'Looks like the jail buddies are the talk of the town.'

'Things started getting worse after Soham's death anyway. A kid raised by an old man would not have much understanding and wisdom.'

'We have two criminals who are talking to each other right now. The only difference is that one lives in the correction centre and the other lives in his house,' Manav said and Pradeep immediately agreed.

'But if we don't want the situation to worsen, we need to take the matter into our own hands. We can't let our families suffer. We wouldn't want our kids to be in the company of criminals. I can't let my innocent Aarav get spoilt because of some idiots who are living around us,' Manav said.

'With due respect to Roshan uncle, I don't think we should shy away from expressing our feelings. I don't know what's wrong with the entire family, but I saw a transgender entering his house that day, late at night. He was there for around half an hour,' Lakhan said, shocking everyone.

'What do we do?' Pradeep asked.

'We do what needs to be done. We discuss it with him and express our concerns,' Manav said with authority in his voice.

'But then, with whatever is going on around with him right now, the time is surely not right,' Lakhan said.

'We'll wait for a few more days, but if things keep getting worse, we'll have to voice our opinion for our people's safety,' Manav said and the others agreed.

Times were changing and so were the people. The street that people loved the most, was slowly becoming a battleground. Love was fading way and once again, past experiences were winning over the present. The society which propagated equality, was bonding over discrimination. But this time, the target was the people who probably needed the most support from their own Beverly Hills members.

Roshan was unaware about the politics which was brewing around him. His grandson Shaurya was laughing like before. He had a new friend who not only supported him when he needed it the most, but also cared for him deeply.

The way Shaurya and Trisha were interacting with each other, one thing was sure! Old, decadent relationships were dying and new ones were blooming.

'We've done a couple of night dates already.'

'You call them dates?'

'Few things to eat, beautiful yellow lights, a specially lit bonfire, warm conversations and that romantic music forcefully put up by my Dadu! If this isn't a date, what else would you call a date?'

'Let's figure it out. Together?'

'Yes. Can we do it like normal humans in the day time or evening for once?'

'I can try. How about day after tomorrow?'

'Sounds like a plan to me already. You go and take a good night's sleep. I'll go and do my morning exercises,' Trisha said.

As they both hugged each other goodbye, they didn't want to leave each other. It was a longer hug than usual. Roshan was watching it all from a distance and was getting all excited about it. He changed the music to more romantic tunes, embarrassing them further.

That's what happens when you speak your heart out, you feel connected, you feel that you belong to each other. And when that happens, timing too doesn't bother much. In love, you have to sacrifice a lot of things. And when it comes to the day boy and the night girl, timings might or might not match, but the love blossoming between the two shouldn't be jet-lagged.

21
Perception Game

The month of January brings two things with it every year – first, the New Year celebrations and second, hopes for a brand new start. After a few months, Roshan started to jog once again. Previously, he would mostly go out with Lakhan's father, but the schedule got disturbed, so Roshan started taking a walk alone.

Roshan was taking a casual walk at the park. He looked around to see if anyone was around. Then, he saw Lakhan's father who was incessantly coughing from a distance.

'Should I start the countdown already, Kamal?' Roshan reacted on his coughing.

'The man who's lost in his own world isn't allowed to speak here. Next time if you take such a long break, you will be thrown out of the park,' Kamalnath replied, moving closer to Roshan and hugging him. He looked visibly happy to have him around.

'I hope all is well at home now. How is Shaurya coping up with everything?' Kamalnath asked.

'Yes, all is well now. He's proven innocent. We have seen some of the toughest days,' Roshan replied.

'Strangely, no one asked me about his well-being before. Everyone must be busy, I guess,' Roshan said. He dismissed his own thoughts as they started taking a walk around the park.

'I am sure it'll take some time. Maybe they just want to give him some space,' Kamal replied. They both saw a couple of people from Prayas lifting weights in the park's open gym. Kamalnath signalled Roshan to leave, but Roshan asked him to stay as he wanted to exercise some more.

Roshan saw those two people for the first time and as Rashid saw him, he offered Roshan the 10 pounds dumbbells. Roshan politely refused to lift those weights and asked him to pass the 2.5 pound ones.

'I'll just do light exercise.'

'Is there a baby doing weights?' Sangram turned to see the person who had asked for the light weights. He was surprised to see Roshan. They both looked at each other. At first, it seemed like Roshan was offended with his comment, but it gradually moved to confusion, then to amazement and ultimately laughter.

'Roshan Kothari?'

'Sangram Yadav?'

They both nodded and hugged each other with a hearty laugh.

'Careful! I am not lifting 25 pounds like you! My body has turned weak,' Roshan said.

'What are you doing here?'

'I own a house here. I should be the one asking you the same question,' Roshan asked and realized that he had probably touched on the wrong topic.

'Well, I loved your society so much that I murdered a person to spend thirteen years in jail, hoping that maybe, one day, I'll live in a correction centre that would be opened in

Beverly Hills,' Sangram said. Roshan and Kamalnath tried to put up a fake smile.

'I need to leave, Roshan. Got something urgent to finish,' Kamal said and left within no time. Sangram and Rashid sensed their discomfort.

'One more reason why people are scared of criminals like us. We don't know what to speak and when?' Rashid said as he finished his set of exercise and offered his hand to Roshan.

'Rashid!' he said.

'Roshan!'

'It has been twenty years that we saw each other last. I remember your son was taking you for a late night drive because you complained to him of not spending much time with him. Does he give you enough time now?'

'No.'

'That's the thing with kids! They get so busy with work that they don't know how to manage their professional and personal lives. So, do you still complain?' Sangram asked.

'Worse! I can't even complaint now. He's gone a little too far.'

'Has he moved to US like the other kids?' Sangram asked. Roshan's painful smile was more than enough for him to realize what he meant.

'Oh, I am sorry. I mean, it's shocking.'

'I just have my grandson to live with now. Shaurya Kothari.'

'Is he the same Shaurya who was there in news in the last few days? I also heard a lot about him in Beverly Hills.'

'Yes, what a way to introduce him.'

'I am glad he's out,' Sangram said as he put his hands across Roshan's shoulder. Initially, Roshan felt a bit hesitant, but then, he felt comforted.

'I've always known you as someone who stayed calm even in the worst situations. Don't mind me asking, but what brought you here?'

'I killed my son-in-law for torturing my only daughter throughout her marriage. He had an extra-marital affair and was so proud of it. He spoilt the life of my princess and then, he was physically abusing her every day. The law could not help me much as he was an MLA's son, so I sacrificed my life to get justice for my daughter,' Sangram said. Roshan was taken by surprise. He looked stunned, but was also proud of his friend.

'This society is harsh. It only teaches you to suffer. We don't even have rights to stop someone from killing us. I mean, we can't request a murderer to stop by folding our hands. If we don't kill them, then we will be killed. Law may not be on our side, but that doesn't mean we let our kids die,' Sangram added. His voice captured the love he felt for his daughter. Roshan could only imagine what his old buddy Sangram had gone through.

'We all have our stories which just don't fit into the right side of our society. But, we deserve a second chance. Rashid's son was blackmailed so harshly, that he fell into depression. One fine day, he decided to hang himself, but Rashid stopped him. Out of frustration, Rashid's son Mehran killed the blackmailer, but since he had a family to look after, he got scared. Rashid took all the blame upon himself. He was in prison from the last eleven years and Mehran didn't even come to meet him! It was because his wife asked him to stay away from his dad who was a murderer, which was not really true,' Sangram said. Rashid had tears in his eyes.

He is craving to meet his family, especially his granddaughter, but he'll probably never be able to see them again. Not everyone who's behind bars is really guilty, Roshan. And our society needs to understand that.' Sangram said.

'You guys have been through a lot.'

'What's worse is that people are still not accepting us. If I ask someone what they would have done had they been in our situation, 9 out of 10 people would say that they would do what we've done. But still, they won't accept us,' Sangram said as all of them walked towards the exit gate of the park.

'I am sure people will change their perceptions about you. It would just take some time,' Roshan said. Sangram noticed that all the families of Beverly Hills were looking at Roshan with disgust. They had anger in their eyes, fear in their hearts and a lot of thoughts going on in their head. They all saw Roshan, but ignored him.

'Now you'd know how difficult it is to change perceptions. I hate to say this Roshan, but you need to get ready for the worst to come,' Sangram said, pointing at the reactions of the people of Beverly Hills.

This street of Beverly Hills was struggling because of the perception game. The members of Prayas were not given a second chance. The kids were not allowed to talk to Shaurya because of his drugs case. Sridharan, because of his old image, was completely boycotted by almost everyone, and Zainab never messaged Roshan back because of her own presumptions. Roshan also forgot to message her after that night.

But you know, when the game of perception gets worse? When everyone starts believing that their perception is the correct one, without paying heed to other sides of the story!

22
#Shauhr

Shaurya finally switched on his mobile after many days. Surprisingly, he saw that many of his friends had unfriended him on Facebook and unfollowed him on Instagram. But one person had started following him everywhere – Shaheen.

"We need to meet up", "Call me urgently", he received a string of messages from Shaheen, which finally got delivered. Shaurya was unable to comprehend the desperation behind so many messages. Before he could grapple with this thought further, he got a call from Shaheen.

'Hey man, you might not know me, but I am Shaheen, Mehr's boyfriend.'

'Why would I even want to know Mehr's boyfriend?'

'You wouldn't, but I need to meet you to discuss something important,' Shaheen said. After a lot of hesitation, he decided to meet him. He kept thinking about why Shaheen would want to meet him.

Is it related to the drugs case? Is it something related to Mehr? Or is there a new surprise life has planned for me?

He kept thinking about Shaheen, his days spent in jail, Trisha and his own deceased parents. He missed them being around. In the last few years, Roshan never let him feel alone even for a second, but after spending a week in prison, he felt all the more lost and heartbroken.

Why wouldn't he? People who had always loved him more than their own kids had now started giving him a cold shoulder. The torture of the prison kept haunting him, which disturbed his peace more often. His Dadu tried to help him through meditation and self-help books, but nothing was helping him heal. His mind kept travelling between a lot of things.

And suddenly, the bell rang. He opened the door to see Shaheen, standing at the door with a fake smile on his face. He looked nervous. Then, he entered inside the house without even asking for permission and got seated on the sofa.

'So, how have you been?'

'I am okay.'

'So, what's going on?'

'Can we please skip the formalities and directly jump to why you are here?'

'Are you sure?'

'More than ever.'

'I need your help.'

'Regarding what?'

'Regarding Mehr. I want you to, kind of, mentor me in loving her.'

'And why would I do that?'

'Come on! You two were perfect! How special the two of you were when you were together. How #Shauhr was better than #Meheen,' Shaheen said. It took Shaurya a while to process what he was hearing. Frankly, he thought that Shaheen must be some stud, but the way he was behaving right now, changed his opinion.

'You must have talked to some other Mehr and not the one who was in a relationship with me. It is because you're saying exactly the opposite of what Mehr used to tell me when we were a thing,' Shaurya said. Shaheen didn't say anything for a while.

'So I might not be able to help you out.'

Shaheen still didn't say anything.

'Take care of yourself. See you some time,' Shaurya said, expecting for him to leave, but Shaheen still didn't say a word.

'She says that the only big thing that I have is my car,' Shaheen said and started crying comically.

'She expects me to perform every time. Even cricketers do not hit a century every time they play,' he added. That reminded Shaurya of Mehr's two minute Maggi noodles comment.

'Oh, that's sad. That surely must have hurt,' Shaurya replied. He also felt a little happier about the fact that Mehr had found someone else who was incapable of sex as well.

'It does. Every time we go to bed, it feels like a knockout match that I am playing. I might look like a stud, but I never really got a chance to get into anybody's pants before,' he said and Shaurya made a disgusted face.

'You could've explained it better.'

'That's what she says after having sex every time. She says that she wants to push me to perform better, but little does she know that it's only making me nervous. My bed time has drastically dropped from 3 minutes 23 seconds to 43 seconds now,' Shaheen said at the risk of being judged and added, 'Okay, decrease 5 seconds of putting the timer on.'

'You put up a timer every time? Who are you? A person getting into bed or a fucking athlete?' Shaurya said.

'That's what she said, are you a fucking athlete that you're running so fast?' Shaheen said. 'I just get very excited whenever I see her undressing herself. It's like I can't believe that she's finally mine.'

'What do you mean by "finally mine"?'

'I've been trying to get her from almost half a year and the efforts finally paid off.'

Shaurya looked a little disturbed to figure out that she left him because of Shaheen and not because of their breakup. That's the thing with breakup and sex; you always keep figuring out what went wrong.

'What do you expect from me?' Shaurya dodged the other details and finally asked him.

'I want you to be my boyfriend-in-law.'

'Is that even a term?'

'We would make one, if there isn't any. Don't disappoint me by saying no. However, I would like you to help me with the things that I should be doing in my relationship with Mehr so that we don't have a breakup, just like you two. But you seem to have moved on.'

'How can you be so sure of that?'

'Remember in the elevator? We were kissing, and it seemed to have no impact on you,' Shaheen said. The mere thought of kissing Mehr again turned him on, but he didn't seem to be in love with her.

'I would like you to sleep over it and get back to me. If there's a salary or any remuneration we could decide for the same, I'll be happy to do so,' Shaheen said in a typical HR style.

'Are you out of your mind? You're offering me money to help my ex love you?' Shaurya said and he looked miffed at his craziness.

'Not only money, as I really want it to work out for me. So if you need any help, just give me a call. I'd expect you to revert before tonight,' Shaheen said. After shaking hands forcefully, he left.

For some reason, this entire conversation with Shaheen left a smile on Shaurya's face. He kept laughing for the next few seconds, until he received a message from Roshan that raised his eyebrows.

'I am going to be late tonight. Have a date to go to. Take care of yourself and I might pick up one of your suits, so don't mind.

He smiled once again and replied with a text.

'That's like my old man! Wardrobe is all yours. Don't forget to carry the protection.'

'Don't be so over-friendly. You're talking to your Dadu and not your friends. Roshan messaged and Shaurya smiled.

While the two generations were coming together in the Kothari house, the generation gap was increasing in Arora's house over a really hot topic which had garnered a lot of attention in Beverly Hills.

23
Family Clashes

Manav Arora, an influential business tycoon, had been receiving accolades and awards from across the globe. People in the industry would listen to him to understand the further trends of automobiles. He had always been the person who would put his professional life first, over everything else.

He always wanted to be there for his son and his family, but he was too busy minting money, that is why he neglected his loved ones.

That night, at the dining table when the entire family was having dinner together, Manav thought of catching up with his kid, Aarav.

'Hope you're enjoying your teenage years. You'll soon be in senior college. What are your future plans?' Manav asked as he served yellow daal and roti in Aarav's thali.

'Yes, very much. Planning to pursue my graduation from Canada. I've heard that there are a bunch of good universities there,' Aarav said, as he put the roti back in the container and replaced the yellow daal with black daal.

'Canada? There are better universities in India. Why don't you apply to them?'

'Which university?'

'What course do you want to pursue?'

'Exactly my point! You're just suggesting that there are better universities, but you don't even know my preferred course?' Aarav said as he started eating.

'You could've said this in a better way. You didn't have to be rude,' Manav said and looked at his wife Soumya, but she didn't say anything.

'I want to pursue a degree in music from Canada and then have a career as a musician.'

'There are many music pandits here. I also know a couple of reality show judges. Learn music from here and then, I'll try to get you in the reality show. You can easily pursue your hobby.'

'It is not a hobby. I want to make a career in music.'

'And who would run my business after me? Shaurya?' Manav said mockingly and laughed. He expected others to laugh with him, but they didn't.

'Why not? He's smart, capable and he's your dead friend's son,' Aarav replied. He wanted to give a sharp response, considering the kind of ignorance Shaurya was facing from the Beverly Hills.

'Yes, the new druggie in town is going to run my business,' he said sheepishly and winked at Soumya.

'He has a name, papa. Stop calling him that. I understand why you randomly picked his name out of nowhere.'

'And why are you suddenly coming out to support him?'

'Because he is innocent and you shouldn't judge him for something that he hasn't done. Also, even if he did it, there are others who are doing it too. You wouldn't know even if your best friend is doing it.'

'He has broken the law. That son of a bitch, Sridharan bribed Roshan to get friendly with the criminals in the center in exchange for Shaurya's bail. You stay away from this. You're too young to talk about it. In fact, you stay away from Shaurya too.'

'I won't.'

'What did you just say?'

'I said I won't stay away from Shaurya, no matter who tells me this.'

'Behave yourself, Aarav. That's not how you talk to your father,' Soumya said.

'And that's not how a father talks to his son! He's just imposing some useless rules and I am not going to follow it.'

'I would've slapped you so hard right now for disobeying me. But that's not something I would do. I'd warn you to stay away from him. I don't want you to create any troubles for yourself, me and my business.'

'Even if you slap me papa, I am not going to distance myself from Shaurya anymore, because I believe he's innocent. He is just being framed for this,' Aarav said as he ate another spoon from his thali.

'It's time you stop believing in rumours and stop talking to those idiots who spread it.'

'What you did that day to Sangram and Rashid on the road was also not very humble. For the kind of background you come from, stop being too snobbish,' Aarav said. Manav slapped him hard for the very first time in his life. Soumya tried to calm both of them down, but the matter was already out of hands.

'You lost all the leftover respect I had for you,' Aarav said.

'I'll go to Canada and never see your fucking face ever again.'

'You're not going to Canada.'

'I am going to Canada and there's no one who can stop me from doing so. I have someone there who loves me at least.'

'Who loves you there?'

'Riddhima!'

'She's your cousin. Are you out of your fucking mind, Aarav?' Soumya shouted.

'I don't fucking abide by any rules that you impose upon me,' Aarav said.

'The way you're misbehaving, it surely looks like you're close to Shaurya.'

'Stop with your outdated thinking already, papa. Go and open the third drawer of my wardrobe. You'll find enough weed and cocaine to get arrested for life. Stop schooling others and me. You don't know anything,' Aarav shouted and cried aloud.

'Forget about this! You don't even know your own son's eating habits. I don't eat yellow daal and roti. That's something I have been following since the last four years. You're so lost in your world that you just don't care about others,' Aarav added.

Manav held Aarav by his hands and locked him in his room.

'You're not coming out of this room until you apologize for your behaviour,' Manav said, his eyes looking furious.

There's a thin line between controlling and disciplining, and Manav had crossed that today.

Beverly Hills had never experienced such serious and loud fights between a son and a father before. The street was shocked, scared and angry because all of them thought that the sudden change was because of the criminals who were staying in their vicinity.

We always like to blame someone if things don't go as per our plan. That's what was happening at Beverly Hills.

And here, for everything that was going wrong, Prayas was the easy target to be blamed. Life at Beverly Hills was surely changing. The street, which was known for cordial relations, was turning into a bunch of people who were selfish, arrogant, and very opportunistic.

24

Shaurya planned a brunch date with Trisha. He looked nervous. He wanted things to go right on this date. He was looking into the mirror again and again. He kept changing his clothes over and over. When he was wearing formals, he felt like trying casuals; when he put on casuals, he liked formals better. He finally made it a combo of blazer and chinos to give it a semi casual look.

They both decided to meet at The Bay View directly. Shaurya, being the over-excited guy, reached a few minutes before time and checked the seat he had reserved for the date.

The waiter kept coming and asking, 'What would you like to order, sir?' Shaurya kept waiting.

After waiting for almost an hour, he placed an order for himself, constantly calling Trisha. She didn't pick up the call at first, and then her mobile was switched off.

Shaurya, who had been very excited for this date, had started to feel frustrated by now. All that had happened with Mehr started coming back to haunt him. He was getting uneasy with every passing minute. The waiter finally came over to him again, telling him that they'd be closing soon.

Just as Shaurya was about to settle the bill, Trisha came running from the other side of the entry. Looking at her, it seemed she had run straight from her bed to reach here.

With a shallow breath, she reached closer to Shaurya. She gulped down his entire glass of water to calm down. Then she sipped lemonade from his glass and said, combing her hair back with her hand, 'How do I look?'

'Perfect for the date,' Shaurya laughed and said.

'I am so sorry I got late. I am not used to getting up at this time. You know how this medical condition works. I put ten alarms, even then couldn't get up. I don't know how to apologize for this but…' she said and paused to scan his face, 'This is the best I could do.'

Shaurya just smiled and said, 'I am glad you could manage to come! This date is as imperfect as we are. I am suited in semi-casuals, you're still dressed in what looks almost like a night suit. I am done eating and drinking a lot of stuff and from your face, I can say you're still hungry,' Shaurya said and it started raining all of a sudden.

'I think god is also enjoying the contrast we flaunt. Showering love upon both of us,' Trisha said as she gracefully ate.

'The situation is very much like our connection. Random, but beautiful.'

'So what are we up to? Where are we going with this?' Trisha said hinting at their connection.

'Somewhere. That is unknown to you and me so far. I've seen plans failing, we should rather just go unplanned,' he said.

Trisha replied, 'I like your choice of words. They get so interesting and beautiful sometimes that one just wants to agree and do nothing else.'

Shaurya just smiled and Trisha asked, 'Can we go down to the beach and enjoy the walk if the date is still on?'

'Absolutely!' Shaurya said as he settled the bill. They walked down to the beach as the rain kept getting heavier. He had never seen Trisha being so expressive and happy before. It was like a moment of truth for both Shaurya and Trisha.

'Why don't you take your jacket off and be a little more casual?' she said and he followed. Shaurya kept looking at her face as they moved towards the waves. Once closer to the water, they started playing like kids. They were playing with whatever they were getting hold of. Trisha was dancing like a kid – shouting, running. She herself didn't realize that she had started crying while dancing.

It took Shaurya a few seconds to register that she was crying and missing her family. Shaurya hugged her and she kept talking about how they used to come to this beach every Sunday. How his father would bring her a candy, how her mother would teach her to make a beach house and how her sister would always beat her in running. She kept crying and even in the heavy rain, her tears were clearly visible.

Shaurya didn't say anything, He was just doing what he could've done best – listen. As Trisha settled down a bit, she hugged him even tighter and kissed him. Her lips were rubbing against his lips. Just after the quickest pause, there seemed to be an avalanche of feelings. They hugged each other tighter and deepened the kiss. They explored each other's bodies, touching, feeling and letting it sink in. They were away from the sight of people and that gave them more freedom.

Soon after, they were fully engrossed in each other. It wasn't just a girl and a boy making out. There were two worlds coming together that evening and the rains were celebrating their love.

Shaurya was looking at the different tattoos on her naked body and Trisha was loving the purity with which Shaurya was making love to her. They themselves did not have any idea how this date would end. But the way it was going, nobody was complaining.

After close to half an hour, they put their clothes back on.

Trisha just said one thing. 'Your girlfriend was a liar. You aren't quick. You like to stay.' She winked at him and it made him super proud of himself.

He had needed this self-assurance. He thought of complimenting her back, 'You were beautiful yourself.'

Trisha replied, 'You don't have to necessarily compliment me back, but thank you.'

What happens when a day guy and a night girl meet each other during the oddest hour? Answer is, they make love in the evening and make it memorable for both of them.

25
What if

Roshan and Zainab finally got in touch and decided to meet up. Zainab booked a cruise for them to meet. Roshan, after wearing one of Shaurya's best suits that suited him perfectly, reached the cruise that started from Taj Hotel, Mumbai.

Roshan looked a little nervous. He was consistently checking his hair, beard, perfume, the crease of the suit and was practicing a perfect smile. The last time he had prepared himself like this was when he was meeting Neeru for the first time. He expected Zainab to be the exact copy of what Neeru was like.

He walked in and saw Zainab standing there, closer to the edge. She was enjoying the beautiful view which the sea had to offer. He kept walking towards her. With every step, he was reminding himself of how much he had loved Neeru. There couldn't be any other woman whom he could love so much. On the other hand, he was making himself understand that it was okay to love a woman who looked like his wife.

As much as he wanted to get close to her, he also wanted to run away from there. The game of desire and guilt was going strong. But as he saw her, he felt something that he hadn't felt for a long time. He saw an elegant beauty who was standing in a red and cream saree. Her earrings were complementing her spotless skin. She wore a beautiful matte lipstick and looked anything but seventy. She didn't look exactly like Neeru, but her eyelashes, her smile, her body-type and her voice made Roshan feel nostalgic.

Roshan had never seen a woman as perfect and elegant as her.

'That's the beauty of the sea. You leave everything that was bothering you behind, and embrace everything that is new.'

'Or you just look back and enjoy the view that's left behind. And think about how beautiful it was when you were there.'

'Then you'd be standing there someday and watching this cruise go. You would think, how beautiful it was when you were here.'

'Well, that makes sense. And knowing how beautiful this moment is with this gorgeous lady, I'd readily give up on some of my beliefs. I would like to go ahead with your conviction. So, can we just hug and end this debate here?' Roshan said charmingly.

'Absolutely,' she said and Roshan hugged her.

'It feels so good to hug someone affectionately after so many years.'

'And it feels good to be hugged by someone who values the person he's hugging. By the way, you look no more than a seventy year old.'

'Thank you. And you look no more than a pretty fifty.'

Zainab laughed a hearty laugh and said, 'No, I am not crazy enough to be called young. I might or might not look fifty, but I know I am the best 70 one can get!' She said and winked at him. That wink reminded Roshan of Neeru. She had winked at him at a few occasions in their relationship and he could never forget that.

As Roshan was standing there with Zainab, he kept thinking about that dream of Neeru where she had asked him to move on. 'Thanks for everything that you've done here. It's the best date I've ever been to in the last forty years,' he said.

'How many dates have you been to in the last forty years?'

Roshan started counting on the fingers and said, 'None.'

Zainab smiled and they both sat on a beautiful red coloured couch. She was wearing a black opium perfume and Roshan was wearing Versace Pour Homme. They both complimented each other together. As they saw the city going away from them, they started opening up to each other.

'I wonder if there could be any better date than this. Everything is so peaceful,' Roshan said as he looked around with a bright smile on his face

'I believe that when we want to know a person, we can't let the noise of people and the city distract us. It doesn't allow us to be ourselves. Sometimes all you need is to breathe and do nothing else,' Zainab replied.

'Yes, the noise of the city might take away some heartwarming conversations too,' Roshan said.

'If given a chance to live a life, I'll prefer to live somewhere between the sea, around all the beautiful sea creatures. Isn't it strange? They say our planet is covered 70% with water and yet we can't live there?' Zainab replied.

'Probably they want some place where they can remain untouched. Pious and pure forever, so that we can enjoy a moment like this,' Roshan said.

'So, how does it feel to go out on a date with an eighty-five-year-old person?' Roshan asked.

'You focus on the age of a person and I value the personality and character. It feels good so far. I like skipping formalities so I'd ask, what do you expect from me?' Zainab said as she smoked a cigar and offered it to Roshan, who denied it. That was probably the only thing that wasn't Neeru-like in Zainab. Neeru used to hate people who smoke and didn't even like standing with them for passive smoking.

'I expect us to be good friends,' Roshan said to Zainab's question.

'There's a lot of difference between what you think and what you say. If only you would be a little honest with yourself, it would make more sense. Let me be that person who doesn't judge you. You can speak your heart out in front of me,' she said and filled a glass of scotch. 'This might help.'

After hesitating for a while and hovering over topics like his past experiences, family and life, they finally picked the most favourite topic – love.

'I feel I haven't been loved enough to have any memories of love. That's why I always keep searching for it in my past. Whenever my wife and I would talk, she would always cut me to other topics. It didn't feel much when it started, but gradually it all started piling up. I'd surprise her with dinner plans, vacation plans and family plans, but that never seemed to make her happy. We never had marriage counsellors back then, so it was always our parents who would try and patch us up,' Roshan said with a tinge of agony that seemed to be unravelling for the first time in years.

'But instead of improving the situation, it worsened it. We were just two people living together who had nothing but a kid to live for. Throughout my marriage, I kept trying to make her happy, and she kept searching for reasons to be unhappy. I am sure no husband would ever say that to his wife, but I even asked her to have an extra-marital affair if that made her happy, but she disagreed to that too. If I had to sum up my life in one word, it was a chase to be loved by the person who didn't love me back,' Roshan said and regretted it the next second. He was cursing himself from within. His relationship with Neeru wasn't perfect, yet he was trying to find another Neeru in Zainab, although still bitching about Neeru to Zainab. 'What an ideal start to this date,' he thought and cursed himself.

'What made her so rigid?'

'She loved someone who was dead, and all her life, she just waited to die. You should've seen her serene smile when she was dying. That's the commitment she had for her love. Imagine the intensity of her love. She was just thirteen when he died, and we got married seven years later. I always wanted to ask her if she could love him and me equally, but then, I thought I would be insulting her love. It might detach us further. She loved a dead person and lived with it. I also wanted to experience it, so I kept loving her for years, even after her death. Now I understand, she wasn't wrong at all. One could live with someone's memories.'

'So, she was a person who used to live in the past?'

'Not always! Her love was in the past, but her life was in present. This created an imbalance in her life. When I started living in my past, she hated that the most.'

'Probably because she thought that it would end your life in a similar way that it did for her.'

'Maybe! These are some maybes for which we're never going to get answers. We are eventfully forced to live with could bes and what ifs,' Roshan said. His melancholic voice reflected his guilt at not asking many questions that he could have asked her.

'It took me a few years to finally make peace with it. And when I did, I lost my son and daughter-in-law in an accident. I am just left with my grandson, Shaurya, who was wrongly put behind bars in a drug case, almost a week ago. The same week when I didn't reply to your messages. I was having a hard time saving my last reason to live,' Roshan said. His tears were in sharp contrast with his smile. Zainab hugged him, which made him feel better.

'I am not going to say that life is going to get better for you because it might not, but I will tell you to stay strong, as you have always been,' Zainab said. 'You might die after that anyway. You're already eighty-five,' Zainab jokingly said and it cracked him up too.

'That's my story! What about you?' Roshan asked.

'Not very different from yours, but I parted ways from my hypocrite husband and children as they did not respect me and my choices. I've lived my life with enough dignity to live the rest of it on my own. So they might not be dead physically, but they're dead to me. Trust me, it makes me so happy to say that I am living the life I always wanted for the last ten years,' Zainab said and smiled.

'It surely feels better when you leave everything that was bothering you behind and embrace everything that is new,' Roshan repeated the same lines that Zainab had said when they had just met.

'When we start living in a moment, we stop worrying about the past and the future. That's how it should always be. Cherish the present moment. We might have better moments, but this moment will never come back,' Zainab said. Then she kissed Roshan. It made the moment a little awkward for him.

'I forgot I had lips all these years,' Roshan said and Zainab laughed with all her heart. Roshan was still feeling uncomfortable and was under guilt for kissing someone other than Neeru. It took him a while to understand, but the last time he had felt so alive was when he had kissed Neeru. He kept reminding himself of the dream from that day to get rid of his guilt.

The cruise was sailing exactly like their lives, with a few ups and downs. They sat together as Zainab rested her head on his chest. In that moment, Roshan realized that one thing that he was missing. It was a sense of belonging and love in his relationship. She could hear his heart beating rapidly, but his breath was calmer, which he had yearned for long.

That evening for Roshan was a mix of awkwardness, happiness and nostalgia. Neeru's words kept ringing in his head again and again. 'Stop living in the past.'

If the world would see them like this, it might make fun of them. But they would also know that the search for true love is ongoing, even when the knees get weak and the hair turn grey. True love can knock at your door anytime.

The music of seventies was playing in the background, but they were feeling young at heart once again. Roshan, for a minute, wanted to forget everything from his past and carry on with the present. But as Zainab rested her arms and head, Roshan kept thinking about Neeru and the last time she had sat like that. He couldn't help it, as if stuck in a maze of his memories.

Zainab was ready to live in the present, but Roshan – though it seemed he was trying to move on – he was still stuck in the prison with bars of the past.

26
New Guests

A couple of months passed and a lot of things changed at Beverly Hills. Lakhan lost his father and suffered from financial loss as the stock market turned around completely after Indian government officially announced the boycott of Chinese products. Manav's company, that had a Chinese backhand, suffered a huge loss too, as they withdrew all the invested money from the company all at once. Rahil, who had got a break in films that propagated the message of spreading harmony between India and China, also ran out of distributors after the recent update. And Sridharan became the MLA of the constituency that included Beverly Hills.

Rahil, the heartthrob of all the girls, was rumoured to be gay. Aarav was forced to take admission in a Mumbai college after his love affair came out in the open. Mehr asked Shaurya to accept her back in his life, but Shaurya was busy guiding Shaheen to win her over. Shaurya and Trisha became thick friends. And Roshan and Zainab were meeting at least once a week to know each other better.

But one thing that still remained unchanged was the relationship between Roshan Kothari's family and the entire street. In fact, it went colder when the MLA announced a victory rally from Beverly Hills. Sridharan, who did numerous rallies before, decided to start the victory rally from Roshan's house. Numerous cars, bikes and the party workers reached the correction centre sharp at 7 in the evening. Beverly Hills was looking more like a party office with flags and hoardings all around, than an elite high class society.

The party workers started sloganeering before Sridharan himself entered and the residents of Beverly Hills looked clearly miffed with it. The police was guarding the place to ensure that no violence happens.

The only people who were happy with the turn of events were the residents of Prayas who believed that Sridharan had given them a second life. As he entered, the slogans kept getting louder and louder. The chants of his name were hurting the residents of Beverly Hills. When he entered with a smile, his supporters showered flowers upon him and he greeted everyone with a smile and joined hands.

He asked the driver to stop his open jeep. He got out to take Roshan's blessings. With a smile on his face, Roshan hugged him and gave his best wishes. The driver took him and the others to Prayas. When he reached the stage, Sridharan touched the feet of Sangram and Rashid, the eldest prisoners as a gesture of respect. He asked the sloganeers to relax a bit as he started the speech.

'When I was a kid, the first thing I was taught in school was how A was different from B, and B was different from C. I grew up a little and then, I was taught how boys are different from girls. Eventually, I started to observe how people discriminated between Hindu and Muslims on the basis of religion.

'I always thought, why, in a country which is known for unity in diversity, everyone is teaching us only about differences and not about similarities?' Sridharan said and the party workers clapped. They started chanting his name once again.

Sridharan, in a very politician-like style, asked them to calm down and continued, 'I thought of serving the underprivileged people. I decided to dedicate my life to ensure that everyone is treated equally. That's when I resolved to celebrate similarities in a world where people were emphasizing on differences.

'In a world where people promote anger and fear, I'll spread love. In a world where people talk about crimes, I'll talk about improvement. In a world where people talk about dividing, I'll talk about uniting. To celebrate the six-month anniversary of this correction centre Prayas, I am glad to announce that the second batch of people from jail will also be brought here. We have seen some incredible results in the past few weeks. A big thank you is due to all the residents of Beverly Hills, who welcomed them all as a part of their family and showered them with love and peace.

'The world in changing rapidly and when this world will be left with peace and harmony, people will thank Beverly Hills for showing faith in our brothers and sisters when no one else did. The existing group Prayas will be released in a few weeks. It's time we welcome the next batch of five prisoners who are going to be released due to their excellent conduct. They are ready to be welcomed back by the world,' Sridharan said and a police van stopped in front of Prayas.

There were people stepping down one by one. The residents of Beverly Hills had never felt so disgusted with Sridharan and his political tactics. Party workers were clapping as they welcomed the prisoners to Prayas. As the fifth person came out of the van, Trisha was shocked. The warmth of her eyes was replaced with intense rage. It might have gone unnoticed by the entire world, but Shaurya spotted it.

Why wouldn't she be angry? She had just seen her father, Mukesh, who had abused her mother for years and finally killed her. She kept shouting and her anger was visible in her eyes, even though so many years had passed since her mother's death.

The street of love was filled with hatred, disgust and anger. The families were feeling helpless about their future. No matter how much they hated Sridharan, they couldn't control his actions. He was an elected MLA in the region now. His master plan of opening up a correction centre, just a few months before the elections had paid off.

He was here to stay. He was more powerful than before and if his records were anything to go by, he was not going to stop here.

27
No Scope for Redemption

The storm had still not settled as the new prisoners were sent to Prayas. The old prisoners were happy that they were just a few weeks away from getting released. But they were also very nervous about starting their new lives.

What would they do? Will people give them a second chance? Will their own family accept them? These were the kind of questions lingering in their minds.

Some of them were happy that their friends were here. A lot of them were bonding over the lost times. The others, who were just weeks away from release, were confused.

'Now that it's almost over, what would you do once you're out?' Sangram asked Rashid and the others who were sitting together. They also waited for him to answer.

'I'll run an institute where I'll teach how to handle bullies. A lot of people commit suicide and the rest of them live out of fear without complaining. It's not good. I want people to stand up for themselves and be capable enough to tackle bullies effectively,' Rashid said, trying to fix a fan by himself.

'I'm almost eighty and not even a thirty-year-old can beat me. I want everyone to be strong and self-reliant,' he added. Everyone looked really impressed.

'What about you, Sangram?' Rashid asked.

'I don't know! I'll probably teach daughters to be brave. I might need your help there, Rashid. I don't know how I am going to do it, but I'll make sure that our daughters and granddaughters are stronger than ever. They should be bold and self-reliant.'

'Maybe just teach the sons how to behave and the rest of it will follow,' one of them said.

'Along with teaching our sons, I'd still make sure our daughters are brave. I want no daughter to get physically abused by her husband. If I find anyone like that, I'll probably kill him and die in the jail peacefully,' he said and the rest of them just nodded in a yes.

'What about you, gentleman? You still have six months to search for your answer,' Sangram asked Mukesh, who looked very lost.

'I'll ask my daughters if I was wrong in killing my wife. I committed the crime because she didn't pay any heed to the warnings when her boyfriend was raping my daughter for three long months. I'd like to ask them what else could I have done in that situation? I'd like to ask them what would they have done if something like that happened to them?

'I'd say that I regret what I did and will live with it for the rest of my life. But I would also like to know what should I do now to get them back in my life?' Mukesh said and started crying like a kid who was in pain for years and finally got a chance to vent it all out.

They all comforted him and Sangram said, 'There's nothing right or wrong, it's not like my crime was more serious than yours, but it is still a crime. I hope your daughters understand the reason behind your actions and can see your guilt. You have every right to ask for an apology.'

They were all silent for a while before one of them asked Trisha, 'What would you do once you're out?'

'I'll tell my father that I am ashamed to have him in my life. I'll tell him that there's nothing you can do to redeem yourself. I'd tell him that killing my mother wasn't the correct solution. I'll tell him that I was equally livid and I punished the culprit, so there was no need to kill our mother. I'll tell him that you died for me, the day you killed my mother. I'll slap him hard enough and tell him that you totally deserve to rot in hell, you fucker.'

Trisha jumped on her father and started beating him with loud cries. Others jumped in to save Mukesh from her. The rage within her came out all at once. In that moment, she was ready to go to jail for another ten years, if she got an opportunity to kill her father.

It came as a startling revelation to many that her father was none other than Mukesh. He came from another jail and this was the first time she was seeing him, after ten years. She kept yelling at the top of her voice and her abuses were heard by everyone on the street. She kept beating him before the guards and other prisoners came to rescue Mukesh.

'Why did you kill mumma? Why did you not think even once about how much she really loved you? Why do you just think about yourself all the time?' She kept crying when people held her back. After crying and repeating those words for hours, she slept.

That night, Trisha saw her mother in her dream where she asked her to focus on the present. She said that there was a beautiful life that was waiting for her. When she got up at midnight, she felt as if she had really met her mother.

That's what happened with Trisha. She kept searching for her mother in different places. Sometimes she would just read some lines behind some auto and think that it was her mother signalling her to do something. At times, she saw her in her dreams where she would try to pass on her wisdom. At times, she would just talk to her when she was alone. Even the wind passing by would mean that her mother approved of what she had asked her. She found her mother in the sun, moon, rains and at times, just in silences.

When you lose the only person you love and trust, what else would you do!

28
Young at Heart

A few weeks later, early rains had started to surprise Mumbai. It's that time of the year when people don't want the rain to stop, for all different reasons. Some don't want it to stop because they want to miss their office. And the rest don't want it to stop because of the dash of magic it adds to the licensed romantic month.

Roshan also did not want the rains to stop because he had planned a special date with Zainab. And what's better than a thunderstorm to grace the occasion!

It took him more than three hours to set his old Ambassador up that morning. He washed it, oiled it and after the basic drill, it started. It was ready to be his ride for the day. He got dressed and as he gave himself a final look, he sat there to do what he enjoyed the most. Just watching the rains and see the world stopping! He always said – when it rains, all the ego drains. The world comes to a halt.

It's raining cats and dogs. It better be a good surprise, Roshan. Zainab messaged and Roshan smiled.

I believe so! It's something close to my heart. Roshan replied back.

Then what are you waiting for? Your lady is ready. She messaged back. Roshan started his Ambassador and as he took it out, he got a few fabricated smiles from the people on the street. It was Rahil who said, 'Are you sure of this ride, uncle?'

'Very sure of it, Rahil! Thanks for asking though.'

'Drive safe and don't collect the pieces if it falls midway,' Rahil joked and Roshan laughed.

Despite everything that had been going on, Rahil hadn't broken his ties with Roshan in the last few months. The other people just greeted Roshan formally, but he knew that their equations had changed after Shaurya's drugs case and his friendship with Sangram.

Roshan had always been the kind of person who would never clarify his stance if he believed that he was right.

He didn't pay heed to anything around him as his mood was very cheerful today.

An oldie chose the most romantic day for the most memorable date of his life. He played his favourite seventies melodies in his car, which surely set up the evening for a retro date.

Zainab was surprised and elated as Roshan greeted her. He escorted her to the car. 'I've never seen an old man who is as romantic as you are.'

'Let's throw our age labels away at least for today. I am not in a mood to feel old tonight. In fact, I feel younger than ever.'

'I have never seen a date that starts so romantically in the past seventy years. You have my heart, Roshan. You have made my life so exciting!'

'As I said, let's throw away the ID cards for a while,' Roshan said and a beautiful song *Mai shaiyar toh nahi* graced the beautiful lady as the car started. As they reached the location, Roshan looked around to see if there was anyone watching them. He parked the car at least a hundred metres away near the garage, so that no one could spot them.

It was raining torrentially and it seemed that it wouldn't stop anytime soon. They walked towards the location. Zainab got scared a couple of times, but she had faith on Roshan. She was shocked to see the location. It was Regal Theatre that had closed twenty years ago.

Roshan reminisced about how he had enjoyed the last show with Neeru in the theatre. Due to the business dispute between two brothers, the court gave them notice that the land could not be used unless the issue was resolved. The case was still running in the court and the two brothers, who had filed the case, had died few years back. Now, their kids were fighting the case.

Roshan took the keys out from his pocket and opened the theatre. He switched on the light from inside and picked the broom to clear the dust. Zainab was shocked to see what Roshan was doing. He looked very excited as he did this.

'I'll give you some time to settle down. Feel at home,' Roshan said and Zainab, who was just looking around, was absolutely speechless.

'You didn't mention "a mad person" in your Binge Date bio,' she said and Roshan laughed. He carried a bag with him and signalled her to follow him towards the projector room.

'Well, I am the treasurer who preserves precious things. The two families fighting for this theatre never enter this beautiful cinema hall, but I still manage to get in once in a while.'

'How come?'

'I bribed the watchmen as this theatre closed because Neeru and I had lots of beautiful memories here. He gave me the spare keys and here I am. It isn't as easy as it sounds. I almost got caught the first time around, but now I know the drill. So here we are!' he said and Zainab looked at him in amazement.

He kept showing Zainab around, describing every nook and corner, as if the theatre was an old friend.

Roshan said and opened his bag. He took out the DVD of *Pakeezah* and after struggling with it for a few minutes, the movie started on 70 MM screen.

Zainab looked surprised at what Roshan was doing for the last one hour. He spread a red carpet there and asked for her hand. He escorted her to the theatre where they both sat as the movie started.

Zainab kept thinking about the guy whom she was dating. Either a lunatic or a passionate lover could do this. He could've gone to the five-star beach resort or taken her for a beautiful vacation date. But she failed to understand why he would do something like this.

However, she felt very special. No one in her life had made her feel like this.

'There's popcorn to enrich your experience,' Roshan said and Zainab kissed on his cheeks. She had tears of joy in her eyes. She tried hard to stop them, but her smile was conveying everything.

They kept watching the movie for a few minutes before Roshan excused himself for a while. He wanted to use the washroom.

'Don't leave me alone, I am scared here already.'

'What are you scared of? We're the only two people here. I'll quickly come back,' Roshan said and Zainab agreed.

She kept looking around the theatre. She was amazed to notice that every seat in the balcony had dates and *Roshan-Neeru* written over it. What surprised her the most was that there were at least twenty dates written in the last five years. That meant that Roshan never really stopped coming here because it reminded her of Neeru. She looked around a little more and saw that almost every seat had *Roshan-Neeru* written over it, but all of them had the same date, *19th June.*

Zainab was confused, scared and clueless. Or maybe it was difficult for her to comprehend the kind of love he had for his wife. She remembered his words on the cruise and it kept ringing in her head.

She loved a dead person and lived with it. I also wanted to experience it, so I kept loving her for years even after her death. Now I understand, she wasn't wrong. One could live with someone's memories.

She immediately walked out from there, but then, she saw Roshan who was standing there at a corner with a cake that had "Happy birthday, Neeru" written over it.

She looked hurt and angry as she said, 'What's all this, Roshan?'

'I was missing Neeru as it's her birthday today, so I thought of spending some time at one of our favourite places.'

'Why would you call me here then? You could've come alone,' Zainab said as she started crying. 'Why did you involve me?'

'Please try to understand, Zainab. This place was a special place for Neeru and me. I wanted to make this place special for both of us now. I wanted to end this first before I begin something with you. That's why I called you here.'

'Roshan, the way you prefer to live in the past, this isn't going to end ever. You're too much into it already. Don't drag me into this. Your behaviour scares me. All of this isn't romantic, it's horrific. Do you understand? You don't love your past, you're obsessed with it,' Zainab said as she walked away with tears in her eyes. As she left, Roshan's hopes of being loved also seemed to be fading away.

Roshan, who looked disappointed, sat there cluelessly for the next few minutes before he came out and drove back to his home. He seemed lost and wiped his tears. Zainab, on the other hand, was heart-broken and once again, alone in her own world.

That's the thing about two different worlds coming together! You know the side you have liked, but there's much more to explore when you dive deep. And many a time, it gets suffocating!

29
The Last Ride

It was a full moon night. Rahil, who was just back from the last day of his shoot, was sitting at the backyard of his villa. He was looking at the stars and counting them in his mind. He thought about the last time he sat like that in his balcony. Deep down, he knew the answer. The last time Rahil sat like that in his balcony was when he had lost his parents. Even though he spent time with them, he was always alone. He always thought that his parents didn't love him enough. They got separated when he was young, so he felt a void in his heart. He did not have a happy family. That is why he always connected with Shaurya whenever he was feeling low and looked after him. He knew exactly what he must be going through.

There was a different sort of calmness to that night. He didn't have any complaints as he felt close to himself more than ever. The breezy wind was soothing his heart and soul. He couldn't have asked for more as he kept staring at the stars. Suddenly, Aarav walked in.

'Dude, where are you lost?' Aarav said as he removed his shoes and sat besides Rahil.

Rahil didn't reply, continuing with counting the stars.

'What are you doing?'

'Trying to achieve something impossible,' Rahil said with a serene smile on his face.

'Are you counting the stars?'

'Trying to! Have counted two-hundred approximately.'

'Has anyone ever tried to count it?'

'Why do I have to wait for someone else to do it first? Why can't I be the one to initiate?' he said as he looked at Aarav for the first time.

'Dude, you could have said it without looking at me. You must've lost the count,' Aarav said and he offered him a cigarette.

'I've quit smoking and everything that kills me slowly,' Rahil said. As he offered him some water, Aarav looked surprised.

'What brings you here?' Rahil smiled and asked.

'I don't know. I just thought that there are a lot of nasty rumours floating around, so you could use a friend maybe,' Aarav said hesitantly as he rolled his cigarette and started smoking.

'Those aren't rumours, it's true,' Rahil said as he started roaming around in his backyard, looking at all the plants. He began to set them up with the cutter. 'I am gay,' he added.

Aarav looked shocked. He was holding the cigarette in one hand and biting his nails on the other.

'I didn't know that.'

'Of course you didn't,' Rahil said. 'In fact, nobody did! After people got to know about it, they fired me from my own show, considering that it would hamper the TRPs.'

'I wouldn't deny, but it surprised me, as you're such a popular and a good-looking actor, any girl would fall for you. Why are you attracted to guys ?' Aarav said as he smoked the next puff.

'You don't have a choice there. It surprised me too, considering that you're young and handsome. You could get anyone. Then, why did you choose your cousin from Canada?' Rahil replied as he took a dying plant out.

'One-all. Agreed with your point,' Aarav replied.

'My definition of love was always unconventional. So, when true love came into my life, I didn't care about social norms. The gender of an individual doesn't really matter to me,' Rahil said.

'Why would people fire you just because you're gay?'

'We live in a society where we preach honesty, but accept lies and social pretension. We like sensationalizing things that do not fit within the popular understanding. The idea of being different is a crime in our society,' Rahil said as he looked around his garden, which looked very neat and organized.

'Weird! How does it matter which hole you want to seek pleasure from?' Aarav said. Rahil felt disgusted at his comment and furrowed his eyebrows.

'Perhaps, I put it the wrong way. What I meant is, your personal choices should not be anyone's concern. But, doesn't it bother you that you've been fired just because of your sexuality?' Aarav clarified.

'I have lived with it for more than a few months now. It has stopped bothering me,' Rahil said, moving inside the house. He kept cleaning the house and arranging things that were scattered.

'Are you going somewhere?' Aarav asked as he saw Rahil organizing everything in the house.

'Yes.'

'Where to?'

'Wherever. Not here. I've not thought about the destination so far,' Rahil said as he started folding all the clothes in the wardrobe and rearranged it properly.

'The way you're preparing everything, it looks like you're off to a long journey,' Aarav said as he saw Rahil locking everything in the house, for once and for all.

'You can spin my toy till I come back,' Rahil said and handed over his car keys to Aarav.

Aarav looked happy, surprised and confused. 'Why would you give it to me?'

'Come on! I've seen you looking at my car, the way Ranveer looks at Deepika. You asked for a ride before and I couldn't give you that. You're mature now and have been a good friendly neighbour. Plus, I never had a younger brother. Consider it as a luxury of having an elder brother,' Rahil said. He washed his face, wore his favourite black shirt and cream pants and clicked a happy, smiling selfie of himself.

Aarav had never seen him this happy and relaxed before. It seemed as if a new Rahil was standing in front of him. He had always seen Rahil shouting, fighting and fighting.

Rahil asked Aarav to take a selfie with him, and they both smiled.

'Why would you do that?'

'You'll need it buddy! When I'll become a star someday and when people would stop judging me for my sexuality,' Rahil said and smiled and as he took one final look around his house.

'Even though I might be a little late in returning, don't let the spirit of selfless love die in our street. They are way better than people who are living outside.'

'Roger that!' Aarav said and thanked him for the car. He began to leave, but came back to hug him.

'There are still good people alive on our street. If you keep behaving like this, you can venture into my list of friends soon enough,' Aarav said and Rahil laughed it off.

Rahil selected two pictures to upload on Instagram – his cheerful selfie and the other one with Aarav. He was very sure of what he needed to put as a caption to these pictures.

> *This is how happy I feel right now. This is the smile I wanted to have on my face throughout my life. But it doesn't always go your way and I accept that. The plans of life are generally different from what we expect them to be.*
>
> *I got immense love from my fans and received hatred from a lot of people who found out about my sexuality.*
>
> *Love, for me, was always an illusion. It always appears from a distance and as we get closer, it disappears. I always craved for love since my childhood, and when I found my soulmate, I realized that I deviated from the norms of the society. I didn't know that I belong to a world that could not stand someone who unapologetically chose to live life on his own terms. I didn't know that when we talk about love, which happens to be so emotional and profound, the biological truths can play such an important role.*

I am happy that I arranged everything in my home today. It didn't feel messy. In fact, it felt as new as it was when I first stepped into this house. Many a times, I tried to achieve the impossible, but when I started counting the starts tonight, I realized that certain things will always be impossible. I've always been in the closet and as I post my last message, I would like to accept that I've been in love with @ rishabh.malhotra who has always urged me to come out of the closet.

I am sorry that I couldn't be as strong as the character that I played in my TV shows. This, in no way, should inspire others to give up in life. However, the world needs to start accepting the difference more openly than ever, otherwise, one will always be bullied and might give up in the long run.

This kid in my picture is like a younger brother to me. The reason I am uploading his picture is because he was the last one to meet me. I don't want the police or anyone to interrogate him. I am leaving this world in search of peace that I wish to attain.

Hoping for a better and non-judgemental world in my next life. Adios.

As Aarav took Rahil's car for a spin, he clicked a picture with it. As he uploaded it on Instagram, he saw Rahil's last post that left him heartbroken. He turned the car quickly and almost raced it at the fastest speed. He reached Rahil's house and as he got inside, he saw many people standing there, looking at Rahil, who had hanged himself to death with a smile on his face.

No one apart from Aarav had tears in his eyes. The entire street was busy talking about his sexuality and assumed that he committed suicide because he was ashamed of it. The street, that was known for spreading love, was full of hatred that night. A street, that fought for its people, didn't fight for their own member. A street, that always welcomed strangers till a few months back, lost one of their own.

Aarav couldn't sleep for the next one week, thinking about the things that could be different if he was alive. He kept thinking about his dear friend whom he had lost too soon. It made him feel alone, all of a sudden.

Shaurya and Roshan were deeply hurt. They felt disappointed with themselves as they couldn't read the pain in his eyes. Rahil was always available for Shaurya, so Shaurya felt disheartened that he wasn't there for him when he was going through a tough phase.

30
A Friend Indeed

It had been a week since Rahil had passed away. Shaurya was not able to come to terms with the fact that a person on the street had lost his life, because people couldn't accept his sexuality.

He was checking Rahil's Google page, Instagram, Facebook and other social media handles to understand the kind of person that he was. He was surprised to see that he had initiated a campaign to support Shaurya when Shaurya was behind bars. No one knew about this, not even Roshan.

He remembered how the entire street, who showered support in his absence, disappeared when he actually came back home after he was proven innocent. The only guy who didn't show any support was the first one to call him.

He remembered his conversation with Rahil when he got back from jail. He remembered how he just walked into his room with a smile on his face and sat with him.

'Tough days, champ!' Rahil said

'Yes, kind of,' Shaurya replied as he still couldn't understand why Rahil had walked into his room. Those were the times when Shaurya was in his shell as he chose to remain silent.

'So, what's happening these days?'

'You want me to tell you the highlights of what happened? There's a news channel that's doing that job already,' Shaurya asked, as he did not want to give any fodder for gossip.

'Come on! I stay away from them anyway. By update, I wanted to know what's going on in your life. You are not defined by the last seven days that you spent in prison, but all the things that you've done before that,' Rahil said and Shaurya looked pleasantly surprised.

'Well, I am glad that someone thinks like that,' Shaurya said.

'Now do I have the permission to sit?' Rahil asked almost seriously.

'I am sorry, I didn't even ask you to sit. Please do!' Shaurya said. The formal tone in which Shaurya spoke made Rahil laugh.

'Didn't your girlfriend call to check on you?'

'We broke up long ago.'

'Really? You guys looked great together. Never thought you were going to break up.'

'It didn't think I would ever go to jail,' Shaurya said and Rahil tried changing the topic.

'When did you break up?'

'Been almost six months.'

'You said, long ago!' Rahil said. 'I don't know what's with your generation, but they don't stick around much. I have hardly seen any relationship going beyond one year. Why did you break up?' Rahil asked, as if he still couldn't believe.

'Because I was bad in bed. I was just like two minute noodles for her,' Shaurya said and Rahil didn't say anything. 'It feels like I am fucked completely. Nothing is going right for me.'

'Well, you're breathing so that's the first right thing to tick off. Secondly, 98% of men in the world don't last in bed for more than 40 seconds, so you're still better than them. And lastly, bad memories always give birth to new good memories. 2007 World Cup debacle introduced India to the greatest cricket team and World Cup victory,' Rahil said citing an analogy.

'I don't follow cricket. Give me an example of football maybe,' Shaurya said.

'I don't follow football,' Rahil said and he kept thinking about the right examples to give. 'What I mean to say is that when you're at your weakest, that's an opportunity in disguise to make you your strongest version.'

He kept his hand on Shaurya's shoulder and said, 'Firstly, I trust that you've not done any drugs. But even if you have, just know that there are a hundred million people who do it every hour in the world, including me! So chill,' Rahil said, but that didn't seem to give Shaurya much strength.

'I never had a younger brother and you never had an elder brother. How about we decide to be there for each other in difficult times, where the world stops believing in us and the closed ones show their true colours,' Rahil said and he meant it completely. Shaurya was listening to him very carefully.

'Our lives are not very different from each other. We both lost our parents at a very young age. We both didn't have a strong shoulder to cry on. Your grandpa gave you everything, but I know you still miss your parents,' Rahil added.

'Anyway, the reason why I am here is simple. You have just stepped into adulthood. There will be thousands of challenges you might face and you wouldn't like them, but giving up isn't a solution. I promise that even if you murder someone and the police is behind you, I'll be the one to protect you from everything. So let the feelings of the last one week pass slowly and heal. Then, move on and face the world once again,' Rahil said as he held Shaurya's hands.

'I'll be around in your tough times and I expect the same from you. You won't say anything, but I would understand your silence and I hope you do the same,' Rahil said and hugged him. Shaurya smiled and acknowledged his effort for being there.

Shaurya didn't say it that day, but it surely made him feel good. Little did he know that he was watching Rahil's infectious smile for the very last time. What killed him from within was the thought that he was not there with Rahil when he needed him the most. The street had lost a gem in him.

Shaurya knew that it was going to take him a while to get over this. He noticed tears in his eyes. While reminiscing Rahil's memories, he received a call from Shaheen. He didn't pick it up the first time around and when he called back again, Shaurya picked up.

'Would you let me live with peace?' Shaurya said, but he was surprised to hear Shaheen crying at the top of his voice. He had never heard him like that before.

'She has broken up with me, Shaurya. I did everything to be with her and yet, she left me. She's not taking my calls. I can't live without her. I just wanted to thank you for being there with me all this while. If not for you, I would've died many months back, but I can't take it anymore. I am putting an end to my life. I want to end this emotional torture by jumping from the terrace,' Shaheen said.

Shaurya took his car out and drove it as fast as he could.

'You're not going to do anything like that, okay? If one person in this world doesn't need you, that doesn't mean that the rest of the world also doesn't care for you. You're not doing anything silly to end your life.'

'Who would I live for?'

'For your family and friends, who care about you and for the ones, who love you. Trust me, it's only for the better. You won't have to make those fifteen second videos anymore with her, you would have the world to hang out with. You won't have to pretend to be someone else. You can just be yourself. Trust me, at the end of a breakup, there's a better person waiting out for you,' Shaurya said. He made sure that the conversation lasted for long so that he could reach Shaheen's house.

'It all sounds good, but it doesn't make any sense to me now,' Shaheen sobbed.

'What if I tell you that you're the only friend I have now. With you dying, I'll also die. You're the younger brother I never had. I'll be around in your tough times and I expect the same from you. You won't say, but I would understand your silence, and I hope you do too,' Shaurya said as he recollected everything that Rahil had once said to him.

For the very first time, Shaheen had tears in his eyes. He stood up to jump down. As Shaurya parked his car and ran towards his terrace, he saw that Shaheen had already given up on the idea of suicide. He sat at a distance with peace in his eyes. As he hugged Shaheen, it felt as if he was hugging Rahil.

He had lost a life few hours back, but he had managed to save a life too.

31
The Baggage of Truth

It took Trisha ten years to control her anger, but just in a few minutes, she had lost all her self-control. A complaint was made against her for misbehaving in the residential area. It was no one else but Lakhan who made an official complaint. When they asked Mukesh about his getting attacked by Trisha, he denied the allegation.

In the last few months, it was the first time that residents got a chance to complaint against the correction centre. But considering Trisha's records of the last ten years, she was issued a warning, failing which would get her an extension of her punishment.

The committee asked Trisha to isolate herself for one week as punishment. That had always been the rule of Prayas. They only decided the punishment and the person facing an allegation needed to experience it. The police just overlooked the entire process.

After a week of isolation, Trisha was exercising when she saw her father entering the gym area. Initially, she decided to discontinue her exercise and picked up her protein bottle and towel to go away, but then, she changed her mind and started walking on a treadmill. Mukesh joined her on the next treadmill. It was early hours in the gym, hence there was no one there, apart from these two.

'How long will you ignore me like this?' Mukesh asked as he reached out to her. Trisha kept walking without saying anything.

'That's not how you ignore your father,' Mukesh said. He looked persistent.

'Excuse me? After everything that has happened in the last few years, you think I still consider you as my father?' Trisha said after putting up a fake smile on her face.

'Whatever might have happened, it doesn't change the fact that you're my daughter and I am your father.'

'You're calling it "whatever happened?" Really! You just killed my mother. Your wife… who never really loved you. You were the person who was responsible for ruining our beautiful family we once had,' Trisha said, controlling her anger. She increased the speed of the treadmill from 5 to 6.

'I killed your mother. That's the reality. I am not shying away from it. But shouldn't I be given another chance to live?'

'You have all the chances you want. It doesn't matter to me anymore. Just don't cross paths with me; I don't want to end up in prison for another ten years,' Trisha said, at an even faster pace now.

'You're just like your mother. True to her words. Full of anger and very dangerous,' he said while walking on the treadmill at a comparatively lower speed. His face looked tired and his body looked weak. He had grey hair and his skin looked old and dull.

'Dangerous? Really?' she said with a smile, almost ridiculing his idea of calling her mom dangerous.

'Yes, that's why she's dead and you're alive,' she added.

'It's always good to see that side of a coin which we like the most. Little do we know that there's another reality, on the other side of a coin, which has been kept invisible for years.'

'Now don't start with cooking up a story just to prove that you are innocent,' Trisha spat.

'I am not here to prove anything, Trisha. To be frank, it just doesn't matter to me anymore.'

'Then why are you telling me all this?'

'So that you get to know the reality too. Your father wasn't that bad, as you thought him to be. So that you get to know that your mother wasn't right at certain points,' Mukesh said as he sped up the treadmill.

'How convenient of you to discuss all of this after ten years of her death? At least leave her now,' Trisha said as she slowed down the speed of the treadmill. 'What do you want, Papa?' she added as tears were visible in her eyes.

Mukesh stopped both of their treadmills.

'We keep running in our lives, believing that our assumptions are true. We need to take a pause sometime to re-examine the circumstances. Not even a day passed by when I didn't think of letting you know the truth. When I finally got an opportunity, how could I stay away from this? I've lived enough with the guilt of not telling you the truth. I can't die with that guilt,' Mukesh said and started showing Trisha her mother's personal diary, her pictures in compromising positions and tons of love letters.

'I am sorry that I'm putting you through all this, but, your mother was cheating on me even before you two happened. She was sleeping with her boss every day and even after knowing the reality, I couldn't do anything. You guys always kept asking me about my reasons of turning abusive in the marriage. That's the reason! How far would a husband go to forgive her wife? The limit was crossed when your mother let her second husband sleep with your elder sister for months.'

'You expect me to believe this? Why would a mother do that to her own kid?' Trisha said, showing her disbelief at what Mukesh had just said.

'Your mother was always a giver in this relationship. But after a point of time, when she got separated and lost all ties with us, she got emotionally disconnected with all of us. Not you, of course, as you were always her favourite child. You never really questioned her.'

'That still doesn't answer my question.'

'Your mother didn't want to upset him at any cost, so she let the things happen and didn't object to it. She turned a blind eye for a kid, who always opposed her and favoured me. Now, how could a mother do that to her own child? Your mother was equally abusive as she let that outsider interfere with our marriage. He had a lot of money, but I just had one daughter to take care of. I could never live with the guilt of letting that person live who allowed this to happen to my daughter. If I have to seek justice for your sister all over again, I'll probably kill your mother twice,' Mukesh said and handed over some call recordings between both of them. They were enough for Trisha to realize the ultimate truth.

'I didn't want you to hate the person you were living with. That's the reason I never shared any of this with you. I respected your mother's decision of staying separately with you and then, marrying her lover. Trust me, it was easier for me to let it out than keeping it hidden for all these years. I chose the difficult option so that we could live with some of the good memories. I missed you and your sister every day. I've lived less and died more in the last ten years, Trisha,' Mukesh said as he picked his stuff from the gym.

'I don't expect you to love your father, but I hope you start hating me less after knowing the actual truth,' Mukesh said and left.

That day, a person left his emotional baggage that he had been carrying for ten years, and another person, who kept worshiping her mother, was exposed to a brutal reality. It wasn't going to be easy for her to accept what lay in front of her. She had still not accepted her father for whatever he had done to her mother. It was a fight between right and wrong, and in a situation like this, more often than not, emotions become overwhelming and truth gets sidelined.

She started walking outside the gym and as she put her bag down to sob her heart out in a corner, no one tried to stop her. Because if there's anything that you learn in a prison, it's to express yourself freely despite what you are feeling. Sangram and Rashid went closer to her and hugged her, so that she could vent out her frustration and grief. Sangram felt as if he was hugging his own daughter and Rashid felt as if he was hugging his granddaughter. They all were crying. That's how emotions flow when they are honest.

At times, it feels like prison has more humans than the ones living out in the open world. In that moment, Trisha needed Shaurya the most and Shaurya needed Trisha the most. But the kind of circumstances they were in, they knew it was not a great time to even meet or talk.

32
A Messenger from your Father

After that day, Roshan kept calling and messaging Zainab. but she didn't reply. Zainab wasn't even there at her own home.

There were lots of people who were sitting in the food court. Some kids were playing and others were enjoying their food, but these two people, Roshan and Sehar, were neither having food nor talking to each other.

People were intrigued to see an old transgender. Roshan was just looking at Sehar, who was cutting his nails.

'Don't talk to me if you don't want to, but this isn't a place for anyone to cut nails,' Roshan said.

'Is this a "No-cutting zone", like how we have "No Smoking" zones in malls?' Sehar said and asked a couple of people around. 'Do you have any problem if I cut my nails here?' Sehar added. People replied with a polite no first and then, they got embarrassed.

'You're embarrassing me, Sehar.'

'That's nothing new. You've always been embarrassed to be in the company of your eunuch friend, Roshan. I feel pity for you. The rest of your friends are either dead or a living criminal who are living in the correction centre.'

'How dare you call Sangram a criminal? He has done his period in the prison already. He has suffered enough already.'

'Just like the people who keep calling us *chhakka, hijra* and all other derogatory names. And by the way, we eunuchs have also suffered already, if you've failed to notice. People never want to meet us freely. They want all of us to be some hidden truths of life,' Sehar said and Roshan realized his mistake.

'Is that why you asked me to meet in the mall this time?'

'Not only that! I wanted you to face the reality and open your mind so that you can embrace the future,' Sehar said as he cut his last nail. Roshan didn't utter a single word.

'It's high time, Roshan. It's more like a now or never situation. You keep thinking about the times that you've lost and while thinking about it, you fail to notice that you're losing some more,' Sehar said.

'What do I do, Sehar?'

'Start accepting yourself, Roshan. Let go of your past and accept the present. You'll be a dead body soon enough. Why don't you just move on once and for all?'

'It is easier said than done, Sehar. Those are the only things that keep me going.'

'No! Those are the things that keep you from living,' Sehar said. He almost emptied a can of Pepsi on his face and that left everyone around shocked, including Roshan.

'So, how's everything at home? Young Shaurya must be having good time,' Sehar said with a smile on his face, as if nothing really happened.

'Why the fuck did you do this?' Roshan said, with anger in his eyes. Sehar looked around with a smile. He wasn't disappointed with the way people were looking at them. A eunuch who threw Pepsi on a gentleman. People already considered him a criminal.

'Why are you making a scene out of this? Why can't you think about the good times that we spent in childhood?'

'Right now? Are you fucking crazy? You want me to think about the past when you threw this cold drink on my face?' Roshan said and kept looking at Sehar's changing expression.

'Yes, why can't you live in the past now, like you always do?' Sehar said. Roshan, who understood his point, relaxed his arms on the chair before wiping the cold drink from his face.

Roshan got up and within no time, ran out of the mall, Sehar didn't even bother getting up to stop him as he knew that his friend wasn't going to stop now. He was hurt, but he knew that there was no other way out.

Roshan picked his car and as he reached near Regal theatre, he looked around to see if there were people watching him. There was no one around. Roshan walked inside the theatre and with a red coloured spray, he removed his and Neeru's name from everywhere it was written.

Roshan deleted all their mobile chats that he had saved from years ago. He went to his own flat and set fire to everything that made him remember Neeru. Even though it was difficult for him, he looked more determined than before to destroy everything that was keeping him in the past. He picked up the keys of his old flat of JB Nagar, where he had lived most of the time with Neeru.

He saw that the lights were off. He took out his keys to get inside the house, but as he saw the lights switching on inside, he quickly ran away from there on the other side where he could see what was happening inside. He saw the new owners of the house, Varun and Aditi, playing with their daughter, Mayra. He kept watching them for over half an hour and as Mayra and Aditi went inside to sleep in the other room, he saw Varun sitting alone, trying to wear an old watch. He smelled an old black coloured jacket and wore it. He picked up a pair of old spectacles and wore them as well. He clearly complimented the old men's photo on the wall.

He looked hurt, lost and a guilt was clearly visible on his face as he started typing a message. Roshan was unable to understand what was happening with him. He kept watching around to ensure that he didn't get caught. Varun kept typing a message.

Hi Papa,

I've been missing you a lot more tonight. You know what day it is? It's my birthday today and like many other birthdays in the last few years, I don't have you to celebrate it with. I am sorry that I lashed out at you that night and didn't even ask you to stop when you left the house. I thought that it was just another argument between us. I didn't know that it was the last time I was watching you go.

I thought we would argue, get upset with each other and will hug each other the next day, like we always did. But you got so upset that you never came back to meet your son. This house feels incomplete without you. There's nothing in this world that would make me feel better.

You probably died in an accident that day, but I die every day, thinking about why didn't I stop you? Why didn't I let go of my ego that day? Why didn't I get up and hug you? My guilt is getting bigger and bigger with each passing day.

Every time I message you, I assume that a miracle would happen and you would reply back, but it never happens. This is the hundredth time I am messaging in the last ten years. I am still not ready to give up on the hope of getting you back in my life.

Lots of love,
Varun

Roshan received a message and could not understand what was happening. He had received a message from the same number from which he had been receiving messages before. That too, exactly at that moment when Varun sent his message. Many questions and answers started swirling in Roshan's mind. He immediately ran towards the name plate where "Varun Sharma and Aditi Sharma" was written.

Roshan could not believe the tremendous coincidence that the person who was sending him messages for the last 10 years, hoping that his dead father must be reading it somewhere, was sitting in front of him right now in Roshan's old house – a house he visited numerous times to re-live his memories with Neeru.

An even bigger co-incidence for Roshan was that he was allotted the same number ten years ago, which belonged to Varun's father before his death. He wanted to go inside and hug him right now, but thought that wouldn't be a great idea. Roshan wrote a message.

Hi Son,

I don't know what kept you going for the last ten years, but one thing is certain that you loved your father a lot. I don't know if there's something called coincidence in this world, but you've been messaging a person who also lost his son in an accident. He had the guilt of not stopping them at the last minute, just like you. I never messaged you back in the last ten years because I knew that the day I message you back, I'll have to admit that it's not my son who's messaging me from some part of the world. I preferred to live in an illusion. I also believe that it's the same illusion you also prefer to live with.

I am sorry to break your illusion today. I am not your father and you're not my son, but I am certainly a father who lost his son. And, you're a son who lost his father. Probably both of them are already living happily in another world. It is quite a possibility that they're also discussing about both of us.

Beta, if there's anything that I've learnt in the last eighty-five years, it's to not live in the past. I don't want you to suffer the way I did.

Trust me, your father must be happy wherever he is. He must be proud of you. It was just one bad night that changed your life. But don't let it change any further. This is a trap and the deeper you go into it, the tougher it's going to be for you to come out of it.

One thing I am sure of, if ever you need a father, I am here. And if I would ever need a son, I believe that you'll also be around.

Let's call it a new start. By the way, after wearing his jacket, watch and spectacles, you look exactly like your father. If you want to know who I am, you just need to remove your name plate to read my name.

Lots of love,
A messenger from your father

Varun could not believe what he was reading. He checked the same message and number again and again. There was a different excitement in his eyes. He wanted to call that number, but after reading the message, he wanted to live in reality and not in an illusion.

As Varun kept re-reading those messages, he removed his name plate outside the flat and saw Roshan's name written over it. He smiled and for the very first time in years, he slept peacefully, without any guilt.

As Roshan started his car, he threw his old flat keys from the Bandra-Worli sea link. He sent a "Thank you" message to Sehar.

When Sehar read the message, he knew that his friend was finally ready to move on in life.

But the day wasn't over yet. Roshan received a message from Shaurya that read, *A police officer, along with the drugs team, have raided the house. They've found something really suspicious in the locked room in the basement.'*

33
Timeless Love

Roshan came back home and didn't speak during the entire journey. Roshan was going back to his own room, but Shaurya kept looking at him. There were lots of questions going on in his mind. He was shocked to see his grandmother's clothes, watches and almost all her things lying in a wardrobe as he opened it.

Roshan had tried to claim that he had moved on, but he never really had! Shaurya noticed that his grandfather had written letters to his grandmother every day. It was only after reading a few of them quickly that he realised that his grandfather was still stuck in the past, not ready to move on.

'Why did you do that?' Shaurya asked after dismissing his own thoughts of heading back to his room.

'If you're looking for an answer here, I don't really have it,' Roshan replied without even looking at Shaurya.

'You'd surely have something to say for all the things that you have kept in this wardrobe,' Shaurya was not going to let go.

'Firstly, they aren't things. They are memories of your grandmother and me. Secondly, I didn't tell you because I wanted it to be *my* past, *my* secret,' Roshan said as he looked into Shaurya's eyes for the first time that day.

'You didn't find it strange even for once? Who does that?'

'Someone who always yearned to get love from his wife. Someone who loved his wife more than anything in this world. Someone who wasn't ready to accept her death. Every single day in the last twenty years, I looked at our pictures, our letters and I felt that she's still alive. I lived with the hope that she would read my letter once she got free. That kept me going. I would fulfil all her wishes of helping strangers out and write it in a letter, so that whenever she reads it, she smiles. She was my routine. I wanted to win her over for the next life already. I was silly to think so, but trust me, it kept me going. I loved that part of my world more than anything else.' Roshan cried it out. Shaurya could not hold back his tears and hugged his grandfather.

'I was always there for you, but no one was there for me,' Roshan said and cried out louder this time. 'I've given up on everything that was my past. Today I genuinely wanted to move on for good. I didn't want to get caught like this. I didn't do any crime. I probably did something that not many people will appreciate. I loved her. I loved everything that reminded me of my Neeru,' Roshan added. Shaurya kept comforting his Dadu.

Roshan kept opening his heart to Shaurya. For the first time in the last couple of years, Shaurya listened to his old man talk everything – from love to sacrifice. For the very first time, he felt that he wasn't really available for his Dadu when he needed him the most.

While talking about Neeru and his relationship, Roshan didn't even realize when he slept. Shaurya brought a blanket for his Dadu as it suddenly started raining. Roshan kept talking in his sleep as if he was bidding Neeru a final goodbye, with a smile on his face.

That night, Shaurya not only missed his parents, but he also realized that love has no age.

34
Bidding Adieu

After winning the MLA elections, Sridharan visited Beverly Hills for the very first time. Sridharan was regularly covered by news channels as he was always a target for opening Prayas. He got many death threats and if sources were to be believed, they were sent by elite businessmen living in the city, who didn't like his style of working. He was even provided with Z+ security to avoid any mishaps.

The eulogy ceremony started as everyone from Beverly Hills were present in the community hall. As Sridharan asked Lakhan to start the ceremony, he refused to say anything for regarding Rahil. 'I don't have anything to say for who lied about who he was, all these years. It seemed like he surely got this from his father, who secretly kept sleeping with high profile escorts. I can just hope for him a better life wherever he is.'

Roshan was shocked to hear what Lakhan said. He interrupted and added, 'This is the most insensitive thing I've ever heard during a prayer meeting. Shame on you, Lakhan!'

'With due respect, uncle, a family that roams with eunuchs, deals with drugs should be the last one to comment on anything like this,' Lakhan said with disgust in his eyes. Manav agreed with Lakhan as he nodded his head in agreement. Shaurya wanted to get up and hit Lakhan, but Roshan stopped him.

'Would you like to go first, Manav?' Sridharan asked.

'I would've loved to, but I think I don't have anything great to say for a person who committed suicide. I don't want to set a wrong example for kids. I would like to pass it on,' Manav said.

Sridharan, who visited Beverly Hills on the thirteenth day of Rahil's demise, was the first one to offer a eulogy.

'Rahil and I go a long way. His father Vikas was one of my good friends. When I saw Rahil growing up, I told him that your kid is going to make you proud someday. Rahil always wanted to get into acting. I understood it very early because whenever I visited his house, he always acted as if he was sleeping. He never liked my presence in his house. He thought that I was probably a bad influence on his father. He never liked me and we all know what happened between us when we met last time. But that doesn't make him a bad person. He was a man of his words, a charmer and a person who entertained millions of people for years. All I can say is that we shouldn't be cruel to judge someone based on their personal choices and sexuality. If only we were more cordial, supportive and available for him, we wouldn't have lost him.'

Sridharan said and others kept looking at each other. Shaurya got up to say a few words.

'Not many of us know, but it was Rahil bhaiya who offered his support when I was wrongly put behind bars. Sri uncle surely kept his words and brought me out of trouble, but the person who kept looking after me was Rahil bhaiya.

He was available when I needed him the most. I regret that I wasn't around when he needed someone to talk to. I'll always remember him as someone who'd secretly help you and not boast about it in public. Living without parents and yet living a life with principle gets difficult. He did nothing wrong in all these years. People who questioned his sexuality, are the ones who should be questioned. He was surely an actor, but he'll always remain my hero.'

Shaurya said and wrapped his eulogy speech. He looked directly into the eyes of the other members of the society. Roshan talked about Rahil and a couple of more people just offered the formalities. Finally, when it came to wrapping up the ceremony, Sridharan got up once again to offer the final words.

'May Rahil rest in peace. To honour the departed soul, I would like to do what he would've done if he got a chance to speak his last words. Through his acting, he changed many lives and now that he's no more, I would like to take an opportunity to announce that the government has decided to extend what we've been doing successfully from last eight months. We have decided to open up another correction centre in Rahil's house,' Sridharan said and that initiated an argument within groups. Manav and Lakhan got up and almost became violent, but Sridharan's bodyguards stopped him. They threw both of them out.

Clearly, no one saw that coming. One more correction centre would mean more criminals around the residents. The property rates would further go low. The quality of life would decline and life at Beverly Hills would never be the same anymore.

Residents started abusing loudly. They kept giving open threats to Sridharan, who was hailed as a king of prisoners. He become a life-changer for many out there. It was out in the open now. Lakhan looked with rage into Roshan's eyes for not going against Sridharan. Manav too looked furious.

The street was no longer of people who loved each other. It had become a street of a few strangers who did not care about each other anymore.

The street had not seen the worst till now. The definitions of enemies were changing gradually. And the ones who were ours, were becoming easy targets.

But you know what happens when rage like this goes out of control? It turns into a smile. A smile that's deceptive, just like Pradeep's smile. No one knows it better than the person who hides behind the smile.

Pradeep smiled at Roshan and as he touched his shoulder, he showed fake support.

Then there was Sridharan's smile that smelled of victory. When people were either full of rage or putting fake smiles on their faces, it was getting difficult for Roshan to understand whose smile was fake and whose smile was real.

While watching all of those smiles at one go, Roshan remembered what his mother always used to say, 'Love your neighbours, but never get too close to them. It's easier to start believing them, but it's tougher to lose trust after all these years.'

Sometimes, you trust the ones whom you've just met. But at times, you can't trust the person you have known for years as a neighbour.

35
A Terrible Loss

It was midnight and like many other people on the street, Trisha too wasn't able to sleep. They all had their reasons. A lot of them were scared because another correction centre was getting opened. The rest of them were already stressed over the tiff between the residents.

Trisha had a very different reason for not being able to sleep. She was continuously thinking about what her father had revealed to her. It was getting difficult for her to come to terms with what her mother did. Her faith in her mother shattered in a few minutes and she realised that the person, whom she hated the most all her life, wasn't wrong.

She kept taking a stroll outside Prayas and as Mumbai rains are supposed to be, it suddenly started raining. Trisha ran to find a spot where she could save herself from getting wet. She spotted a big open wooden hut where people would generally sit to chill during the evening. When she went inside it, she was surprised to see Shaurya already sitting there.

'Hey, I didn't know you were here,' Trisha said as he spotted him.

'I'm sorry, I wasn't around when you needed me. I heard what happened,' Shaurya said.

'Come on! We both were dealing with our emotions. My father turned up out of nowhere and you were dealing with a suicide!' Trisha replied.

'What are you thinking?'

'Some questions that don't have an answer. And some answers which I never knew even existed,' Trisha said as she took her jacket out and settled down.

'I don't know what that means, but it surely sounds like trouble,' Shaurya said and offered her a Davidoff.

'Finally, after all these months, I am getting a chance to return you the cigarette you first offered to me,' he said and Trisha smiled.

'You like returning the favour. That's for sure,' Trisha said.

'I like giving everything a fresh start and that's only possible when we close the past completely. Right?' Shaurya said.

'You're asking the wrong person, who has just faced a brutal reality from the past, that she's not yet ready to accept,' Trisha said and Shaurya waited for her to finish. 'I've just found out that my mother had an extra-marital affair. She also let that bastard rape my sister even after knowing everything,' she added. Shaurya kept quiet for a long time in shock.

'What happened? You've suddenly become quiet,' she added.

'I am able to understand you better now,' Shaurya said as he exhaled the smoke.

'My idea of what is right has changed completely, I will be relieved in a couple of days from now, but what do I look forward to? A home full of emptiness where only the sound of death echoes. Can you imagine how purposeless my life has become?' Trisha said with a forced smile on her face.

'I don't know where my sister is? I don't have a mother to go to. My father is here, completing his term in prison. I don't know where to start from?'

'Start from saying sorry maybe? I am not sure how he'd feel, but he certainly deserves an apology from you for blaming him all these years.'

'Wasn't I right?'

'You were right, but he too wasn't wrong.'

'Does that make me a bad person?'

'No, but an apology would surely make you an even better person. You've seen yourself getting angry with your father for killing your mother, but you haven't seen a father dying daily to prove that he wasn't all wrong. If he was wrong, was your sister's rape right? I don't think so, and if you remember, you killed that bastard for the same reason. So when the reasons for killing were the same, how does it make one person right and the other one wrong?' Shaurya said as he smoked his last. All of a sudden, it started making sense to Trisha.

'I guess what you're saying is right. I'll feel better if I hug him and apologise. We can probably shed some tears together for all the lost times,' she said and her face lit up. In that moment, she forgave her father.

She got up and said, 'Probably it's never too late to express what you feel. Thank you, Shaurya.'

Shaurya smiled and she started picking her jacket to go out. She walked a few steps to go out, but then, she returned with twice the speed, only to hug Shaurya. As they looked at each other passionately, she bit his lower lip and started kissing him for all the love that she had lost in the last ten years.

'This kiss was long due,' Trisha said as she smiled and Shaurya, who was still in aura of that moment, couldn't process it immediately.

Trisha picked up her jacket and reached Prayas, only to end the long-going rift with her father. She was there to hug her father and say sorry for misjudging him. She knocked at his door, and as the door opened, she hugged her father like there was no tomorrow.

He kept crying for all the time that was lost. After a lot of hesitation, his hands shaking, he finally put his hands around his daughter to hug her and tell her that he had never stopped loving her.

She broke down completely and started crying, almost howling in pain. That day, a daughter was crying, who couldn't apologize to her father for ten years for misunderstanding him. She couldn't tell him how much she missed him. She kept expressing whatever she felt as she held his hands and kept kissing his forehead again and again in a hope that the clock would go a decade back and their lives would become normal as before.

She wanted to make up for all the lost times with her father. She said, 'I want to start a new and better life with you.'

As Shaurya walked back home that night, he realized he had got the person to live his life with. It was Trisha!

Trisha refused to sleep anywhere else but in his father's lap for the entire night. She kept talking, sobbing, but that was the first time in the last so many years when she slept peacefully during the night.

36
Burnt to Ashes

We all have been taught to consider our neighbours as our family, because they're the ones who are just a knock away.

We all love and fight with our neighbours, but at Beverly Hills, people could get deceptive because not everyone who smiled had the best intentions in their hearts. Not everyone who ignored you thought bad about you. But you know who're the most dangerous neighbours? Who don't speak with you anymore. Once you know that, you need to stay careful.

Roshan was reminiscing about how the street had changed in the last few months. He felt that the street didn't bring people closer anymore. He felt that it was no one's fault, to be frank. He kept thinking about Aroras, Kanitkars and everyone else who were a pillar of support earlier. Little did he know back then, that times would change so drastically. He was wearing a collar in his neck after a sudden jerk. He was struggling with pain. However, the pain of watching the street falling apart was much more intense than the physical pain.

It was 3:30 a.m. when he saw a truck, loaded with luggage, enter into Beverly Hills. He assumed that the truck would stop in front of Prayas, so that more people could join.

Just in the morning, the required arrangements were done and it was named as Prayas-2. Four people from Prayas-1 were already shifted here in the morning, but the truck stopped in front of his house. Roshan signalled the driver to go towards Rahil's home, but it didn't move. Sehar, along with a group of eunuchs, got down in front of his house. He looked surprised and shocked at the same time.

Roshan didn't understand why Sehar was here? But his confusion didn't last long as he saw Zainab getting down from that truck later. When the eunuchs started shifting the luggage inside his house, Roshan looked confused and hopeful at the same time.

As Zainab reached close to him, she said, 'All my life I've suffered. I don't need to tell you why, but I have decided not suffer anymore because I never felt so strongly for anyone like I feel for you. You put a full stop to your past and I am here to walk with you into our future. I've decided to move in with you,' Zainab said and Roshan frowned as he still couldn't understand the reason behind why she was here.

'To solve your confusion, I met Zainab and let her know about what all happened in the last few days. She has decided to live the last few years of her life with you,' Sehar said and Roshan asked, 'How did you track her?'

'I am a eunuch and I can track a new born too. She was still an easier find,' Sehar said. Roshan had a happy and satisfied smile on his face. All the people started dancing with dhols beating around and everyone from Beverly Hills came out to see what was happening.

Like always, a lot of them threw a disgusted look and talked about the old man's fantasies and his friendship with eunuchs. They were clapping and giving them blessings. They kept singing and dancing for minutes.

Roshan took out some money to offer them, but Sehar refused to accept it. Instead, he offered money to both of them and said, 'Roshan, our blessings are with you. You both will have a happy life. *Khuda kare tumhari nazar mujhe lag jaaye.*'

All the eunuchs started offering blessings to both of them. As they moved out into the truck, a huge explosion shattered the neighbourhood.

Rahil's house was under fire. The way the fire was spreading from all sides, it seemed that it had been deliberately started. Loud screaming sounds were coming from Prayas-2. Roshan could hear the screams, fear and cries. Sehar, along with the others, immediately jumped out from that truck. After spreading in all the four different corners of that house, they tried their best to extinguish the fire.

Sehar and other eunuchs saw three people in black hoods, standing huddled, struggling hard to save their own lives. Those people were wearing fire proof jackets, but they didn't look like life-saving now. They looked scared, their body language suggesting that it was their first time. At first look, it seemed they had purposely set this house on fire.

Sehar, without giving it second thought, jumped inside to save whoever he could. He tried saving all the three people who had supposedly set this house on fire. They came out safely and Sehar went inside again to see if there was anyone left, but the fire around him kept growing stronger. Now, it looked almost impossible to come out of it.

People living in the neighborhood got all charged up to save people. They saw the inmates of the correction center and eunuchs trying their best to not let the fire spread any further. They saw them risking their own lives to save their houses around Rahil's. They were throwing water, keeping other people away and evacuating people living in the neighborhood.

Sehar was badly burnt in the fire and breathed his last there and then. Roshan started running to save his friend, but all other eunuchs stopped him from getting into the fire. The street that was known for love was filled with tears, screams and only sorrows.

A eunuch, who had nothing to do with anything, had died that night. Sehar's words kept ringing in Roshan's ears for long.

The three people whom Sehar saved were lying on the road. As everyone came and unzipped their hoodies, they saw Lakhan, Manav and Pradeep. They had set fire to burn down Prayas-2. They knew that the jail authorities were having a meet with all the prisoners in Prayas-1 and there was no one inside. They didn't want to kill anyone, it wasn't their intention, but they definitely did not want another correction centre. They wanted to spread the message that keeping criminals in Beverly Hills wasn't acceptable anymore.

The fire brigade reached and controlled the fire, so that it didn't spread across Beverly Hills. Sridharan reached within a few minutes and the entire street was looking at the new criminals in the town. They were the criminals who had worn suits all their lives, driven expensive cars, kept their kids away from bad influences and judged people on their past and sexuality.

The entire street was looking at them with rage. Roshan lost his only true friend. He did not get the opportunity to convey his gratitude to him, or say sorry for the multiple times Roshan had let him down.

And like Roshan, somebody lost their father, somebody lost their son. But that's not everything that was lost that night. Some people also lost respect. The street that was known for love also lost a reason to be loved anymore.

37

Gift me a New Beginning

It wasn't just another day at Beverly Hills. It was a day when the real faces behind the masks were getting revealed. The people on the street were looking at Lakhan, Manav and Pradeep.

It was early morning for a few and late night for the rest of them. One thing was common for all the people living on the street – they couldn't sleep.

Prayas-2 was burnt to ashes and with that, the ray of hope of humanity died too. The whole street was in mourning as it was converted into a cremation ground. It was filled with police, media, ambulances and politicians all over. The loud sirens were echoing in the street.

It wasn't still out in the open as to who set fire to the building, but the body language of the family of the three men suggested that they would never forgive them for what they had done.

They all gave them dismissing looks and those three sat shocked, defeated, crying. Sangram, Rashid and all other inmates came closer. All other eunuchs were also standing there with them, as Sangram said, 'How weird is this? We tried saving family members of the people who hated us the most! Who probably could've killed some of us.'

'Killing people was never our intention. We just wanted all the criminals to go away from here,' Lakhan said, crying.

'Welcome to the gang! Now you're also a criminal. How does it feel?'

'We just did this to protect our families,' Manav said, looking lost and defeated.

'We also did whatever we did to protect our family. The only difference is that we did it ten years ago, and you've done it now,' Rashid said.

'But we don't want to take any action against you. We've been through the same. You've done wrong and even though we know the emotions you've gone through, nothing justifies your action. But this needs to end somewhere; this whole discrimination between two sets of people. We need to decide when that would happen, and we think it should be *now*. We want to end it here. We don't want you to go through the same cycle that we've been through. We don't want your families to suffer as our families did. The life inside prison is difficult, and life after coming out is going to be tougher. We aren't lodging any complaint against you,' Sangram concluded.

'And we eunuchs have always forgiven people for the way they treated us. If Sehar was alive, he also would've wanted us to forgive you all, no matter what you did. But never expect blessings from us in our life; you've done enough to damage our soul.'

Everyone left from there after that, sad and heartbroken.

The people in Prayas-1 had their bags packed as they were ready to leave after twelve years of their imprisonment.

The happiness of starting their life once again was disturbed by the death on the street.

Trisha, who was standing outside, looked lost, as she waited for the police van to arrive. Sangram and Rashid were just signing a few important papers after completing the term successfully.

Shaurya was shattered, to say the least. As he moved towards Trisha, he didn't know how to start, so he asked the obvious.

'So, you're leaving?' he asked.

'I guess I am. Till a week ago, I was thinking that it's probably best for me to leave, and now when that moment has arrived, I don't know what to do?'

'So where would you go now?'

'I wish I had an answer, but nonetheless, I'll have to leave. I'll probably start with getting all my identity cards back and will get my father's name added to mine. I am glad you gave me a piece of advice that day and it worked well for me,' she said and Shaurya just smiled.

'All this while, I was happy that my father was in jail for whatever he had done. Now that I am going to stay away from him for a few more months, I am missing him more than ever. I am missing the idea of a family,' she said and successfully stopped her tears from rolling.

'Sometimes we never get to know why we do what we do. I am guessing we've no other option but to live with it, like I've started to deal with my parents' death. All these years, I kept telling myself that it was my fault that I couldn't stop them from going. But now, I don't have that regret. It wasn't in my hands and whatever happened with your father, wasn't in your hands either. But you still got the chance to get back to your family. Your father would be relieved soon and he'll be with you, forever,' Shaurya said.

'We all keep living life on our perception. We are so obsessed with our own perspective that we forget that reality could be different from our perceptions,' she said. Shaurya thought if the feelings they had shared in the last few days were just because of their situation, or were they real.

'What do we do when we are confused between our perception and the actual reality?' He asked as he saw two police vans entering the street together.

'We should give sometime to our perception till it becomes a reality. Or if we know about the reality first, we should accept it as there's nothing that can change it,' she said and smiled. She hugged him for the last time before getting into the van. They both had tears to hide from each other. As they held each other's hand, they promised to be with each other. Their commitment could not be captured in words.

And as she turned away from Shaurya, she saw her elder sister, Miesha standing there with tears and guilt in her eyes. She had come with her husband and her two-year old daughter. As they both ran towards each other to hug, Shaurya had a pleasant smile on his face. He was extremely thrilled for his friend.

Trisha was standing speechless. She had nothing to say. She just kept touching her sister and kept kissing her. They both were crying their hearts out. 'Thank you so much for coming back. You have no idea what it feels to have you and Papa back into my life.'

'You should be thanking Shaurya for making this happen. He kept tracking me for months and when he finally met me, he told me your side of the story. He is the one who convinced me to be here. Welcome to the family once again, my baby sister. We need to get over the past and move on to the future now,' Miesha said. As they hugged once again, they looked inseparable. They had tears of joy in their eyes.

A police van welcomed all the prisoners with a flower bouquet, congratulating them on completing their term and on becoming a part of this beautiful world once again. In the meantime, another police van put handcuffs on the elite citizens who had just started their life as criminals.

Roshan and Zainab saw two different visuals – as prisoners who looked like a threat were off to a happy start. And those who this society respected the most, had done an unforgivable crime.

As they both saw the two extremes of life, they realized, more than ever, that it's better to live in the present than dying in the past.

This street had seen it all in the last few months – a suicide because of sexuality, people becoming criminals to protect their own families, a political master-stroke, a young talented guy getting falsely accused of doing drugs, a strong guilt of a daughter after her father's death, a beautiful bond between Shaurya and Trisha when they both became each other's shadows, sunlight and moonlight whenever needed. A person who was always deprived of an identity just because this world's heart wasn't big enough to identify the third gender as one of them had saved the lives of people who had always promoted discrimination. A eunuch doing the best for his childhood best friend and for humanity. This street also saw the love story of the oldest couple they'd ever known.

The departing police van left in its wake, the hope for a new beginning.

A hope that people don't judge each other because of their past anymore, a hope that this world will again someday turn into something that treats a human like a human, a hope that if you're good, this society might accept you someday with open arms and a hope that the hope of new beginnings still exist. Love is there, if you're willing to find it.